IMPACT

CLOVERDALE – BOOK ONE

BRUNO MILLER

IMPACT:
Cloverdale, Book One

Copyright © 2019 Bruno Miller

Find out when Bruno's next book is coming out. Join his mailing list for release news, sales, and the occasional survival tip. No spam ever.
http://brunomillerauthor.com/sign-up/

Published in the United States of America.

What would you do if the grid went dark?

Vince Walker is looking forward to the beginning of the summer and a visit from his son Cy. But while picking up his son at the Indianapolis airport, the country is thrust into nuclear warfare with the detonation of multiple EMPs.

With fires burning out of control and the loss of the electrical grid, the entire country is thrust into chaos. Vince and his son, Cy, are forced to fight for their lives and escape the city as the world they once knew crumbles around them.

As they try to return to their hometown of Cloverdale, Indiana, or what's left of it, they struggle to accept their new environment. Forced to come to terms with the harsh reality of the nuclear attack, they press on through what is quickly becoming a post-apocalyptic wasteland.

Challenged with the absence of utilities and emergency services, they must save who and what they can before it's too late.

OTHER BOOKS BY BRUNO MILLER

The Dark Road Series

Breakdown

Escape

Resistance

Fallout

Extraction

· 1 ·

With a population of just over 3,000 people, Cloverdale, Indiana, was the kind of town where you knew your neighbors. It was the kind of place where it was common to see people out on their porches in the evenings while they enjoyed the onset of summer, although that was changing faster than Vince Walker wanted to admit.

It had been a cold and what seemed like an impossibly long winter this year, and Vince was happy he could drive with the window down for a change this morning. It was finally starting to feel like summer, even at this ridiculously early hour. It was such a cold winter, in fact, that he had been deer hunting just a handful of times last season, much less than the usual, and as a result, he only managed to fill his freezer halfway with venison. He hated to admit it, but the older he got, the less tolerance he had for sitting in a cold deer stand for hours on end.

Vince fiddled with the radio as he drove the route to his shop, just like he did most mornings. Due to a sore back and the need for an extra cup of coffee to get him going, he was running later than what he would have liked this morning. It was still very early—4:15, to be precise. He usually made the drive from his house on the outskirts of town to his garage in Cloverdale about an hour later than this.

But this morning was different. This morning he had to be in Indianapolis by 5:35. He was picking up his son, Cy, at the airport, and he promised himself he'd be at the curb early in case the flight landed ahead of schedule. But more than that, he was anxious to see his son. Although they emailed and usually talked once a week or so, it had been six months since Vince last saw him in person. That was over Christmas, when Cy came out and they did a little deer hunting together on the property out back behind the house.

Vince just had to stop by the shop and meet one of his mechanics, Bill. Of all of Vince's employees, Bill had worked for him the longest, and Vince trusted him the most. He was going to watch the place and look over things while Vince ran to the airport this morning.

Vince glanced at his watch again and checked the time. He should be fine; it was only a couple more miles to the shop. Thanks to I-70 being so close and Vince's lead foot, the trip to the airport would only take half an hour or so.

The sky was beautifully clear and the full moon cast a silver light across the stubble wheat in the surrounding fields. Some of the farms had yet to harvest their crop of soft red winter wheat, which swayed back and forth in the early morning breeze.

Vince finally settled on a talk radio station out of Indianapolis. He wasn't familiar with the station, but the hosts were talking about the North Korean government's recent testing of two intercontinental ballistic missiles (ICBMs). Lately, that was all anybody was talking about on the news. It was the kind of thing Vince would usually ignore and take with a healthy dose of skepticism. As a former major with the 101st Screaming Eagles and a veteran of the Vietnam war, he despised government and politics. He would normally avoid the topic altogether, but it had been all over the news for these past couple of months. These days, relations between countries seemed to be in a constant state of decay. Every week there was a terrorist attack or some other atrocity.

The powers that be seemed more concerned about not offending anyone or their beliefs, and thanks to the under-the-table deals between corrupt governments, the sanctions against offending countries were all but worthless.

Of course, this was all his opinion, and who was

he? As far as D.C. was concerned, he was merely a resident of the *fly-over states*, as they were called. It was like watching a car crash from the back seat. Not much he could do about it.

Then again, Vince lived in Cloverdale because he wanted to be in one of those fly-over states. After his career in the army came to an end, the decision to move back home was an easy one. He was born and raised here, and as an only child, he enjoyed life on his family's farm. His father grew wheat and corn on the four-hundred-plus acres the family owned until it was no longer financially viable. His parents sold off most of the acreage piece by piece while he was away with the army. Every time he came back to visit, the farm shrunk. Now, it was reduced to a mere twenty-acre parcel that included the house he still lived in today.

With each parcel sold and each visit home, he watched his parents' health deteriorate. His father ended up taking a job at the local Chevy dealership while he could still work, and his mother ended up as a secretary for the high school. They seemed happy enough when Vince visited, but he never saw his parents as content as they were when they had the farm.

Shortly before his last tour was up, Vince's mother passed away unexpectedly. Not long after that, his father's health took a turn for the worse. Vince convinced his now ex-wife that they should move to Cloverdale and take care of his ailing father. It wasn't a hard sell. After all, it was a safe and quiet town with good schools. It was the perfect place to raise Cy, who was six at the time. It made perfect sense to Vince; the old farmhouse was plenty big enough for all of them, and this way he wouldn't have to put his father into assisted living. They made the move and things went well for a while—white picket fence and all—but it didn't last.

His ex couldn't handle small-town life. They had lived in and traveled to some pretty exotic places during his army career. It was an almost constant change of scenery from one assignment to the next. He was more than ready for a slower pace of life, and he thought she was too. But she was a city girl at heart, and after a few years, she became bored with Cloverdale and they grew apart.

He found himself spending more time in the woods, hunting and fishing with his son, so he could spend less time at home. When he wasn't in the woods, he was at the garage, where he put in unnecessarily late nights to avoid the inevitable. He knew the relationship was over but, for Cy's sake, he held on for as long as he could.

Vince leaned forward and turned the knob on the radio. He'd heard enough news for a while, and besides, he was only half-listening. He wasn't sure what he believed anymore. Every news outlet had its own agenda to push and changed the narrative to suit its needs. Who knew the real state of affairs anyway? The world was a complicated place, and on this peaceful Saturday morning, the problems in the news seemed a million miles away. He had better things to think about today. Cy was coming to visit.

As Vince passed the place that his wife used to rent when they first separated, he glanced out the window to his left. He couldn't help himself. Hard to believe that was almost sixteen years ago now. He could still picture little Cy waiting on the front steps for his dad to pick him up for the weekend.

Unfortunately, his ex only lived there for six months before moving back to Washington State. They had made some good friends there during his last assignment at Fort Lewis, and she headed back to familiar grounds. Last he heard, she was living near Seattle with her latest boyfriend and selling real estate for his land development firm.

They never talked anymore, and the only information he ever got on her came from Cy. They didn't hate each other, but with their child grown and living on his own, there was no real reason to communicate or stay in touch. And if he was honest with himself, he still harbored some resentment over her taking Cy away from him all those years ago. The thought of it still stung a little, even after all this time. But what choice did he have? Someone had to stay behind and take care of Vince's dad. With no other immediate family nearby, the responsibility was his and his alone.

Vince took a sip of coffee from his insulated mug and swallowed as he tried to wash away the memories. His son would be here today, and he was going to focus on that for now.

· 2 ·

They only had a few scheduled customers today at the garage. A couple oil changes and a brake job, if Vince remembered correctly. No big deal, at least nothing the guys couldn't handle without him. As much as he disliked being open on Sundays, it was too lucrative not to be. Sunday was a big day for walk-ins. It was the beginning of the summer vacation season, and lots of folks would be traveling past Cloverdale on I-70. It was a main cross-country route and was heavily used by trucks shipping supplies across the country and campers toting vacationers in search of adventure.

It wasn't uncommon for some desperate highway-weary father, in need of parts or repairs for his overworked SUV, to wander into the shop on a Sunday afternoon. The wife usually stayed in the car and tried to entertain the rowdy kids while the father explained their situation in hopes of finding a quick fix for little money.

Vince usually felt sorry for them and did his best to get them back on the road as soon as he could. In some ways he found himself jealous of these travelers. He'd never been able to do the big family trips like that. Even when he was a child, his parents rarely took him anywhere, though on occasion his dad would take him to see a race at the International Motor Speedway in Indianapolis. But he never went on any significant cross-country adventures like the ones the people passing through Cloverdale embarked on. They could never leave the farm long enough to get away, and there was never enough money. Or at least that was what he was told as a child.

This only made him more curious about what lay beyond this sleepy little town and fostered within him a desire to travel. Vince yearned to see the world and always had an inquisitive nature when it came to how things worked. These were the things that motivated him to join the army out of high school—that and the fact that he would have been drafted anyway if he didn't attend college. Not really knowing what he wanted to do, he decided that college seemed like a waste of time and money.

He initially learned aviation mechanics in the army before realizing he'd rather jump out of planes than work on them, but his true passion was cars. On the farm, he learned at a young age how to fix things and was always expected to help out when it came time to work on their 1956 Massy Ferguson tractor. Vince never minded helping, though, and those times were some of the best memories he had of his father and the reason he still had the tractor today.

The now antique tractor still ran like the day it arrived on the farm. Vince remembered it well. It was one of his earliest memories. He was five years old and it was a warm summer morning when it arrived at the farm on a large flatbed truck. Vince remembered how proud his father looked as the delivery man unloaded the shiny red tractor. His father seldom showed that much emotion. Maybe that was why he took such good care of it. He kept it parked inside the old barn behind the house and only used it a few times a year. He had long ago let most of the twenty-acre property return to its natural forested state and mostly used the tractor just to do a little bush-hogging around the place and to cut trails to his deer stand. The tractor was also a favorite in the town Christmas parade, and he usually got asked to pull the local 4H float with it.

Vince's mechanical ability served him well throughout his younger years, and the opportunity to take auto mechanics during his last three years of high school only fueled his passion for all things mechanical. It was something the school had eliminated from its curriculum years ago due to budget cuts.

Vince shook his head as he thought about the time he wasted attending every town hall and school board meeting possible. The decision to remove the course had been made, and it served to reaffirm his opinion of government—that the common, everyday person had little say in how things were run.

Growing up, he owned an assortment of cars and trucks and often sold them for a tidy profit once he finished restoring them. It was enough to forgo having a regular job and working at a burger joint or the local lumber yard like most of his friends.

Something about working on cars put him at peace with the world. It was a chance to immerse himself in something and forget everything else. It was something he could do alone, and he liked solving problems. He always dreamed of owning his own shop one day, so when the opportunity came along to buy the local garage in town, he jumped at the chance.

When he and his ex first moved back to town with Cy, he took a job at the same dealership his father worked at. He was thankful for the job, but after thirty years of doing things the army's way, Vince didn't want to work for anybody but himself. The garage was his chance at independence and to be his own boss while doing what he loved.

He renamed the place Major's Auto Repair. "Major" was also the nickname his high school buddies gave him when he returned from the army. It stuck, and that was pretty much what everyone knew him as. He reckoned there were probably some people in town who didn't even know his real name.

Major's Auto Repair quickly established a reputation for top-quality work and honesty, and he considered himself blessed to have enough customers since the day the doors opened. He had enough business to keep three full-time certified mechanics busy. He didn't turn a wrench much himself anymore, and it was just as well. There were plenty of other aspects of running the business to keep him busy. It was also a gas station with a small storefront attached to the repair shop. There, he sold everything from light camping gear and RV parts to snacks and fresh-picked produce — when he had it.

The produce came from the little garden behind his house. He had a plot measuring roughly one hundred by fifty feet, and he tilled it every spring and grew an assortment of vegetables for himself and some neighbors. He sold any extra produce at the shop, although "sold" was probably too strong of a word to use. In a sort of honor system, he put the produce on a table out front and left a can for people to put money in whenever they took something. He didn't mind helping people out if they couldn't afford it; it was better than seeing the vegetables go to waste.

Vince slowed down as he turned off North Main Street and made his way around to the rear of his building. He normally parked inside the fenced-in area out back. There was a rear door that led to a storage room and then his office on the back side of the building. This required him to stop and unlock the chain-link gate that led to the vehicle storage yard. But that wouldn't be necessary today.

Making sure his eyes weren't playing tricks on him, he brought the car to a stop as he leaned over the steering wheel.

"Aw crap!" he muttered. Bolt cutters had chomped through the chain and the gate was partially open.

· 3 ·

Vince reached under his seat for his wood-handled Colt M1911. The .45 ACP-caliber pistol was nearly as old as he was, but it was the gun he was most comfortable using. It had seen him through some tough situations in the past, and carrying it made him feel like he was never alone. He had a permit to carry the sidearm, but with his back bothering him, he'd gotten into the habit of sliding it under the seat while he drove and was sometimes guilty of leaving it there.

Without taking his eyes off the gate, he quickly turned the car off and killed the lights. He immediately regretted the loud exhaust noise that bounced off the building. He should have been more cautious about pulling into the lot, but how was he to know that someone had broken into his shop?

There had been a few break-ins around town in the past few months. The local police department was working on the cases and believed they were all related. Apparently, it was a group that came from out of town between two and four in the morning. But with the interstate at the edge of town and only three full-time officers, the police didn't have the resources to get anywhere further than that.

At least that was what John Rice had told him, and he should know. John was the sheriff in Cloverdale and a good friend of Vince's. They'd gone to high school together, and like Vince, John went into the army. The only difference was that John got out after his tour and came right back to Cloverdale. He lucked into a deputy position here and never looked back.

Vince eased his way out of the car and shut the door without letting it latch closed. He was pretty sure the thieves were long gone, but he had to be careful; it was still early and a little dark out. As he approached the gate, he saw a set of tire tracks in the dirt and gravel. He hadn't missed the intruders by much. If it wasn't for that second cup of coffee, maybe he would have caught them in the act.

Vince eased the gate open with the tip of the gun and walked around to the back of the building. He grabbed his key and went to unlock the door but stopped.

He shook his head. "Oh great. One more thing to fix around here." The thieves tried to force their way in through the back door, and from the looks of it, they used a crowbar and sledgehammer. The metal around the deadbolt was dented and battered. Near the handle, the wooden door frame was broken away from the wall and splintered.

Fortunately, the door and the locks, albeit worse for wear, had done their jobs and held off the intruders. Vince was going to have to replace the door and the hardware. "There goes a couple hundred bucks." Vince rubbed his forehead as he let out a frustrated sigh.

Of all days, this had to happen today. He was hoping for a calm, easy morning so he could get Bill going and get out of here. He would have to call John on the way and let him know they needed to get out to the shop and take a look at what the would-be thieves had done. He was sure John and his guys would want to try and get some prints if they could and figured it would be best to leave the battered door as it was. It didn't look like it would work, anyway; the deadbolt was damaged so badly he doubted he could even get the key in it anymore.

Vince tucked the handgun into his belt and headed to the front of the shop. He unlocked the main customer entrance, which led to the storefront, and flicked one of the wall switches. One side of the store hummed as the old fluorescent bulbs flickered to life, and he surveyed the room for a moment. It was too early to turn all the lights on; half would be enough to see without spoiling his vision for the darker areas in the back of the building. Everything looked as it should have. Thankfully, the thieves had given up at the back door and not tried to smash their way in through the front. At least he had that going for him; the back door would be a big enough mess for him to deal with. He could handle installing a new door and hardware, but one of the plate-glass windows in the front of the shop would be expensive and something he would have to hire out.

Trying to remain grateful for the little things, Vince made his way past the shelves and coolers of drinks. He was about to head into the back of the building and check on the rest of the place when a set of headlights cut through the dimly lit storefront. He recognized the old Dodge pickup with the off-road lights mounted on the front. It was Bill.

Vince really wanted to check out the back of the building, but he thought he better catch Bill before he touched anything and let him know what was going on. He spun around and headed back out the front door just in time to stop Bill from slipping through the gate.

"Hey, Bill. Wait up."

"Hey there, Major. Good morning." Bill tipped his torn and faded baseball hat, which sported the shop's name along with the American flag across the front.

"We had an attempted break-in here last night," Vince said.

Bill stepped back. "Oh, you're kiddin' me! That's terrible."

Vince pointed to the dangling chain on the gate.

"Did they get anything?" Bill asked.

"No, but they made a mess of the back door." Vince led him around to the back of the shop and showed him the damage.

Bill shook his head. "Oh man. Well, at least they didn't get in. Is this the only spot?"

"As far as I can tell." Vince checked his watch. "Look, you know I need to get going this morning, so when one of the other guys gets here, send him down to Mary's for a new piece of chain. Maybe get something a little thicker, and I guess get a new door ordered. But nobody touches it until John or one of his guys does their thing, got it?"

"You got it, Major."

"I'll call John on my way," Vince added.

"Should I get something to block this door off until we get it fixed?" Bill asked.

"Good thinking. Whoever goes to Mary's can get some lumber to secure the door."

Mary Clark ran the only hardware store in town. When her husband passed away several years ago in a bad car accident, most people in town expected she would sell the store and move down to Florida with her daughter. But she didn't. Instead, a week after the funeral, she opened the store and went on with her life. Vince always admired that about her, and he respected her for her tenacity.

If he wasn't picking up Cy this morning, he would have gladly gone to see her himself. They had become good friends over the years, and she was easy to talk to. On slower days, he spent many hours talking with her over a cup of coffee at the hardware store. She was only a couple blocks away, and it was an easy walk from the garage. In fact, he was guilty of making the occasional unnecessary run to the hardware store for a few nuts or bolts just to see her smiling face. He tried to play it down, but it was tough to hide the fact that he had a thing for her. It didn't go unnoticed by the guys at the shop, either, and they never missed a chance to give him a hard time about it.

Bill followed Vince to where their vehicles were parked. Vince paused by his car and pulled the .45 out from his belt and stuffed it back in the holster under the seat in his car. "You got it under control?" he asked.

"No problem. Go get your boy. I got it handled." Bill tipped his hat again, then climbed into his truck and moved it to a parking spot along the side of the garage. Vince waved and got into his car. The engine rumbled to life as he turned the key, and for a brief moment, he forgot about the break-in.

"Soundin' good!" Bill called out over the throaty exhaust note, right before he entered the shop and disappeared.

Vince smiled as he took in the sound and put the 1962 Ford Country Squire station wagon in reverse. The car was one of his never-ending projects, and to the casual observer, it probably didn't look like much, but that was how he liked it.

When Vince found the car at a farm auction some years ago, it was the ugliest thing he had ever seen—in a good sort of way. Complete with the original lime-gold metallic green paint job and chrome accents dulled by years of neglect, the car practically begged to be rescued. Upon closer inspection, Vince realized the car still had the original 390 FE V-8 engine under the hood. He immediately knew he needed to have the car, and he needed to make it go fast.

What the car lacked in looks it made up for in mechanical ability. He completely rebuilt the motor and added a few custom touches of his own. He managed to squeeze 650 horsepower out of the big block engine and wasn't afraid to use it. The last time Cy came for a visit, he had the carburetor apart and couldn't take him for a ride. It wasn't the smartest thing to drive in the snow either; with that much power, it could get away from you in a hurry.

But he had the old wagon running like a top now and was anxious to show it off to Cy. His son would appreciate it. He was a gear-head, just like his dad.

▪ 4 ▪

Vince pulled onto Main Street and headed north toward the interstate access ramp. It was a straight shot up the highway to the Indianapolis International Airport, and I-70 would take him right to the terminal. He wasn't one for the city and didn't care for the congestion or overall dirtiness of the place. He did his best to avoid trips there and was very successful. Other than the occasional airport run, he hadn't been to Indy in years.

He read enough about city life in the Sunday paper to know it was going downhill fast. The headlines alone were enough to deter any sane human being from visiting—at least that was how he felt. Homicides, carjackings, gang violence, and shootings were prominent in all the news he heard and read. There seemed to be a fresh, never-ending supply of violence to fill the *Indianapolis Star*, which Vince received in his mailbox each Sunday. In the years since he subscribed, the crime section of the paper had certainly grown.

Vince navigated the curve on the access ramp and merged onto the interstate. He rolled the window up as he accelerated. The old wagon responded with a throaty rumble and picked up speed. He didn't let off the gas until he hit seventy-five miles per hour. The car was running great, and Cy would be impressed. Vince couldn't help but smile at the sound of the smooth-running engine.

He was grateful that the airport itself was outside of Indianapolis. While it was still crowded and busy, at least he didn't have to go too far into the craziness or drive through any of the bad areas of town, although that didn't stop his blood pressure from rising as the city's skyline came into view. He attributed some of it to nerves. He was excited to see his son but also a little anxious.

Their relationship was solid, but Cy had been struggling lately. Though he was reluctant to open up about it over the phone, he talked about his dissatisfaction with how life was going in more than a few of their emails. He was a mechanic at a custom motorcycle shop outside of Olympia. He didn't have a stake in the place and felt like he was under appreciated and wasting his time there. He had also recently broken things off with his long-time girlfriend, Kate.

Vince could see the kid wasn't happy and thought he maybe needed a change of pace. He debated whether or not he should offer him a position at the garage. It wasn't that Vince didn't want his son there; he just didn't want Cy to think he was doing it out of pity. He also didn't want to limit his son. Cy was a talented mechanic in his own right, although it wasn't what he'd gone to school for. As a graduate of Seattle Pacific University, Cy had a degree in business administration, but like his father, he had a penchant for all things fast, especially motorcycles. Unable to find a job with his degree after he graduated, he settled for doing something he enjoyed: working on bikes.

Vince doubted Cy would take him up on the offer, but that didn't stop him from thinking about the possibilities. Cy could move into the old farmhouse with Vince until he got on his feet and found his own place. They could make up for lost time.

Vince shook his head. He was getting ahead of himself. He promised he wouldn't push the issue and would be careful about how he brought it up. Still, it would be good for his son, and he knew it.

Eventually, someday, the garage would be Cy's anyway. Vince wasn't getting any younger, and it made sense to him. He would plant the seed on this trip and get Cy thinking about it. At the very least, Vince wanted his son to know he had options.

Fortunately, traffic at this hour wasn't horrible. On top of that, it was Sunday. Even the city had to sleep sometimes. The traffic he did see comprised a few delivery trucks running their morning routes and the occasional out-of-state SUV loaded with luggage and getting an early start on the day's driving.

Vince pulled out his phone and glanced back and forth at it until he pulled up John's number. Might as well make the call now while he had a little time to kill.

John answered on the second ring. "Hey there, Major. What's going on this morning?"

"Hey, John. Hope I didn't wake you up," Vince joked.

"No chance of that. I'm over at the diner. They got broken into last night."

"Well I hate to add to your list of problems, but somebody tried to break into the garage last night too. Busted the chain on the gate and beat the snot out of the back door."

"Oh, man. They get in?" John asked.

"No, just tore the place up. Left some nice tire tracks in the gravel too."

John sighed. "Okay, we'll head over to your place after we wrap it up here. I'll see you in a bit."

Vince could hear the frustration in John's voice. He and his deputies were already up to their eyeballs with this mess, and he hated adding to their troubles. "I'm on my way to get Cy at the airport," Vince said. "But Bill's there. I told him not to touch anything."

John laughed. "Okay, well you better get off the phone and pay attention. If I know you, you're doin' about eighty-five right now."

Vince chuckled. "Yeah, yeah. I'll catch up with you when I get back into town."

"All right, talk later." John hung up.

Vince put the phone down on the seat and glanced at the speedometer. John was wrong anyway: he was going ninety.

Up ahead, he saw the exit for the airport and moved into the left lane. Backing off the throttle a little, he took the long curved exit through the large array of solar panels that stretched out on both sides of the highway in long shiny rows. He was always fascinated by the thought of being off the grid and had done some research on solar energy. A couple of years ago, he had a bank of solar panels installed on the roof of the garage. It didn't get him totally free of the power company, but it did provide more than half the electricity they needed to run the shop. They worked so well that he planned to put them on the house but hadn't gotten around to it yet.

As he passed the last row of solar panels, the airport came into view. He checked the time. He was a few minutes early, so he relaxed a little and slowed down even more. There were only a handful of cars in sight as he glanced in the rearview mirror and abruptly changed lanes. He veered to the left and followed the sign that read GARAGE AND DAILY PARKING. Since he was here early, he might as well go in and surprise Cy at the security exit. If he could find a kiosk open, maybe Vince would have a coffee waiting for him.

Vince entered the parking garage and noticed how good the car sounded as the exhaust note echoed off the concrete structure. He easily found a spot on the second level, which was where he preferred to park when he came to the airport. It was on the same level as the terminal and just a short jaunt across an enclosed glass walkway. The place wasn't very busy, and he chalked it up to being so early and a Sunday. He spotted an open coffee shop and ordered a large black coffee for himself. He paused for a second and then ordered Cy a dry cappuccino; that was what he ordered last time he was here at Christmas, when they went to a new bagel and coffee place that recently opened in Cloverdale. Vince barely recognized half the drinks on the menu, so he stuck with his usual, black coffee, just to be safe. In his opinion, the place was too fancy and a little pricey, but he humored his son.

It was going to be so good to have Cy back

home for a while—and maybe a lot longer if he accepted Vince's offer. Either way, they'd get some fishing in and spend some quality time together. Despite the mess back at the shop, Vince was looking forward to the summer.

· 5 ·

Vince scanned the crowd as a group of arriving passengers exited the security area. Cy should be somewhere in this group, and the monitor that displayed flight statuses showed his plane as having landed a few minutes ago.

"Dad!"

Vince heard Cy and then saw him making his way through the crowd. The two embraced for a brief hug as Vince juggled the coffee.

Vince smiled. "So good to see you again. It's been too long."

"Good to be here. I was expecting to find you at the curb."

"I got here a little early so I parked and came in. Is that your only bag?" Vince asked.

"Yep, just the one. Nothing to pick up at baggage claim. We can get out of here."

"Here you go. Dry cappuccino." Vince handed one of the cups to Cy.

"Oh, nice. Thanks." Cy took a sip of the hot coffee as the two began to walk.

"So how was the flight?"

"Pretty good. No crying babies or anything like that. I actually had the row to myself so I could stretch out a little."

Vince looked Cy over and patted him on the back. He was still taking in the fact that his son was finally here. Cy looked a little thin, and Vince wondered if he'd been eating enough. "It's so good to have you here," Vince said. "I've really been looking forward to your visit."

Cy smiled. "Well, I'm all yours for a couple weeks."

"I'm parked close, just across the walkway." Vince led the way through the entrance and to the enclosed glass pedestrian bridge that led to the multistory parking garage.

"So what are you driving?" Cy asked.

"I brought the wagon, but I've made a few changes that I think you'll like." Vince pulled out the keys. He was about to hand them over to Cy and offer to let him drive when suddenly an intensely bright flash of light filled the walkway.

"What the…" Vince and Cy both flinched, and for a moment, Vince thought a plane had crashed, but to his horror, the sudden burst of light was followed by a rumble that shook the walkway, and he knew it was much worse than that.

"Don't look at it!" Vince yelled over the noise. Temporarily blinded, people froze in their tracks. Something big had happened—something more than a plane crash. As the glow of the light faded, Vince heard another rumble and then felt the pedestrian bridge begin to move.

"Run! Now!" He grabbed the other side of Cy's bag and the two sprinted for the end of the walkway.

Cy looked around, confused. "What's going on?"

"I don't know, but it's not good," Vince huffed.

The rumbling was growing louder now. As they reached the end of the walkway and entered the parking garage, they looked back and saw windows shattering in a chain reaction that accompanied the now deafening roar of the once distant rumbling noise. One after the other, starting at the terminal side of the walkway, the panes of glass exploded inward, spraying glass fragments on those unlucky enough to still be in the walkway. The only other sound Vince could hear over the noise was the screams of the people caught on the bridge as they were ripped to shreds by the glass shrapnel. No one was left standing in the walkway. Vince considered going back to help, but as he looked at the bodies and the pooling blood, he realized there was no use. They needed to save themselves—if they could.

Mouth open, Cy stood motionless as he stared at the scene unfolding in front of them.

"Come on," Vince said, grabbing Cy's shoulder and shaking him. "We need to get to the car!"

After a few seconds Cy snapped out of his daze and turned to look at his dad.

"Let's go!" Vince urged.

Cy remained silent but nodded in agreement as the two dashed through the parking garage.

Vince could feel movement under his feet. What could make that much of an impact? Vince glanced back at the walkway and it was gone. Now there was only a gap of empty space between the parking garage and the terminal. Thank God they hadn't gone back to try and help anyone.

Other people in the garage were running around and yelling. Relieved to finally have reached his car, Vince unlocked the passenger side first. He quickly ran around and got in the driver's seat. Cy threw his bag onto the rear bench and buckled in as he stared at the empty space where the walkway had been.

Vince heard more explosions in the distance. They sounded like the first one but lacked the rumbling noise. Bursts of light shone through the partially open exterior walls of the parking garage.

The wagon roared to life as Vince fired it up. He spun the wheels and backed out of the parking spot. He slammed it into gear and the tires screeched again, this time carrying them forward. *Calm down, calm down,* he repeated under his breath as he tried not to panic. Others had found their cars, but no one else was pulling out and leaving. Vince and Cy were the only ones moving, and although Vince felt guilty about it, he was glad; he could quickly exit, descend the spiraling ramp, and leave the parking area.

As they neared the end of the exit, a large crack formed in the concrete column that supported the center of the structure. He mashed down on the gas pedal and sped onto the open road. He felt better now that they were out from under the building, but they were far from safe yet. The road forced them to drive past the terminal, where he would have been if he picked Cy up at the curb like he originally planned.

There were no other cars moving, but people were running everywhere and he had to slow down and swerve several times to avoid hitting anyone. He passed a few cars parked at the curb and saw smoke rising from their hoods. Nobody was leaving. Why? Then it dawned on him, what was going on, although he resisted the thought at first.

Now that they were out in the open and could see the multiple mushroom-shaped smoke plumes rising in the distance from every direction, he could no longer deny the obvious.

He looked at his son "You okay?" he asked.

Cy didn't answer. He was busy staring out his window and taking it all in.

Vince raised his voice a little. "Hey, Cy. You all right?"

Cy turned to look at him and said what Vince hadn't wanted to. "They're nukes, aren't they?" He stared at his dad blankly.

Vince nodded slowly. "I'm afraid so... I think EMPs."

· 6 ·

A loud mechanical whine coming from behind them cut their conversation short. They turned to see a large commercial airliner puncture the roof of the terminal and explode in a ball of fire that obscured the tail section and extended upward hundreds of feet over the building.

Another plane got their attention and landed a couple hundred yards away on the tarmac. Wheels still up, it bounced off the runway and seemed to float in slow motion for a moment before making contact with the ground again. A shower of sparks engulfed the fuselage as it careened out of control down the runway and into the grass. The plane pitched and caught a wing on the ground, spinning it around like a toy and ripping the wing off. It finally came to a stop and rolled onto its side in the trench it plowed through the mud.

Vince thought of the people on board the planes and felt bad for them. He tried to take some consolation in the thought that the passengers in the last plane would probably live. But most of the ones who survived would be badly injured, and that meant they were as good as dead now. Before Vince could give it any more thought, Cy slapped the dash with both hands and braced for impact.

"Look out!" Cy shouted.

A man in a blood-stained suit and with a crazed look on his face ran straight into their lane. Vince swerved just in time and narrowly avoided hitting him. The big Ford wagon heaved to the side and fishtailed with a loud screech as the tires fought for traction on the dry asphalt. Vince wrestled the wheel and straightened the car out.

"Lunatic!" he yelled. He gripped the wheel tightly and focused ahead. After he regained his composure, Vince felt bad for yelling, and it dawned on him that the poor guy was probably blind from the nuclear flash.

"That was close!" Cy turned to watch the man for a second before looking at his dad.

"EMPs?" Cy's forehead wrinkled.

"HEMPs to be precise. High-altitude nukes that create an electromagnetic pulse." Vince kept his eyes trained on the road ahead. They were almost past the terminal; just a little farther and they'd be out on the open highway. He was anxious to get away from the airport and the city.

"You mean like in the movies, where everything shuts down?" Cy asked.

Vince nodded. "Exactly like that."

He swerved again, this time to avoid several cars blocking the right-hand lanes; some of them were on fire now and burning out of control. Cy turned his attention back to the nightmare unfolding outside the car. As they neared the end of the roundabout, Vince saw the open highway ahead and pressed down on the gas pedal. The sudden acceleration caught Cy off guard and forced him back into his seat.

"Whoa! But how are we still running when all these other cars are broken down, and why are they burning?" Cy went back to looking out the window as they passed the last of the smoldering cars parked near the arrivals curb.

"The EMPs create a surge of electricity or a pulse, and by the looks of it, enough of one to cause some circuit overloading. Add a little fuel to the mix and you've got problems."

Just then another loud explosion sounded, and Vince glanced in the rearview mirror to see a large fireball rising from the runway. Another plane had fallen from the sky.

Cy turned in his seat to take it in. "This is crazy! Do you think this is happening everywhere?"

"Let's hope not. They have systems in place to intercept missiles." But as they left the airport and the city behind them, it was obvious that whatever system the government had in place to intercept missiles hadn't done any good here or anywhere else they could see.

Now that they were clear of the airport, Vince surveyed the landscape and didn't like what he saw. There were large black plumes of smoke rising from every direction, some close and some distant. This certainly wasn't the only area affected. It was worse than he thought, but his immediate concern was what he saw behind them—or the lack of what he saw.

Absent from the skyline over the city were the high-rises and office buildings of Indianapolis. In their places, thick, grayish-black smoke filled the air. Visible pieces of debris floated in the chaos. In the brief openings between clouds of smoke, he caught glimpses of a much different Indianapolis. The high-rise buildings that normally reached skyward were now mere shells of concrete and rebar, hollowed out and stripped down to jagged rubble by the force of the blast. The buildings lacked glass and no longer reflected the bright morning sun. He continued to check the rearview mirror, hoping to catch a glimpse of the downtown area, but the thick black smoke had obscured their view completely, and the farther they drove away from it, the less he could make out.

Vince wondered if the same scene was unfolding under each one of the ominous-looking clouds on the horizon. They were scattered across the landscape as far as he could see. He looked over at Cy, who had pulled his phone out.

Cy looked up at him blankly. "Nothing."

Vince turned the knob on the radio and adjusted the dial. As per his expectations, the only sounds were static and a few electronic whines and pops. He checked the AM frequency and got the same result.

How could this have happened without any warning? Scattered throughout the airport where he had been waiting for Cy, there were dozens of TVs tuned into news stations of every variety. Not a single mention of anything: no emergency warning signal, no emergency broadcast interruptions. How could it get this far without anyone knowing they were coming? He knew the U.S. government had a system in place to deal with this sort of thing. Didn't they?

His normal morning routine consisted of listening to the news on the TV in the waiting room of his garage. And lately, with tensions rising between the U.S. and North Korea, the networks seemed to run a constant news feed with updates from supposed experts on the situation. Among the many panels of experts that seemed to saturate the news, he recalled a segment about the ballistic missile defense system (BMDS). He couldn't remember the guy's name, but he remembered his description of the—quote—"failsafe defense system." The man was adamant that the BDMS was impenetrable and that the United States was safe from any North Korean attempt to launch an attack.

According to everything Vince had heard and read in the papers, the North Koreans weren't supposed to have the capability to launch ICBMs, at least not one with a sizable payload. They lacked the technology to put an ICBM on target at that distance, although it wasn't for lack of trying. In spite of supposed sanctions against them, there seemed to be a story or two every week about the North Korean regime and its unwillingness to comply with the United Nations' request to cease and desist its nuclear program.

Of course, this didn't come as a surprise to Vince. In his opinion, the UN was a weak-handed organization that had little bite to back up its bark. Not to mention the impossibility of dealing with the dictator of a regime that starved and tortured its own people.

Among the many things Vince felt right now, the anger stung the most. The politicians and leaders of the world let this happen. Blinded by power and money, they squandered the common man's future. Now they were all doomed to a meager existence of survival of the fittest.

He looked over at his son, who was in a daze and staring out the window. No doubt in disbelief. Vince could barely bring himself to accept it. He couldn't even begin to imagine this turn of events from Cy's perspective. A young man in his twenties was supposed to have his whole life in front of him. But that all had changed in the blink of an eye.

Vince was grateful for one thing, though: Cy was here with him, not stuck in Washington on his own—or, worse yet, thousands of feet in the air on a doomed flight like so many others.

᛫ 7 ᛫

Vince was lost in his thoughts, so much so that he barely paid attention to the burning cars scattered along the roadside.

"Look." Cy pointed to three people and a dog walking along the side of the road about a half a mile up ahead. It was an older couple and a girl with a yellow lab.

"They want us to stop," Cy said.

The man was waving his arms in the air, signaling them to pull over. Vince slowed down and leaned over the wheel to get a better look.

"I don't know… Wait a minute. Is that…? I know them. It's the Morgans." It was Fred and Hannah Morgan. They were distant relatives on Vince's mother's side of the family. They lived over in Quincy, Indiana, just a few miles from Cloverdale.

"Who?" Cy asked.

"Their daughter Reese is around your age, maybe a little younger. She's a distant cousin."

"I never heard you mention them before," Cy said.

"My mother's sister had a daughter, Hannah. We don't really keep in touch, but they bring their vehicles into the shop for repairs." Vince pulled alongside the weary-looking travelers as Cy rolled his window down.

Hannah recognized Vince right away. "Major, is that you?"

"The one and only."

"Oh, thank God," Fred said through labored breathing as he wiped sweat from his brow. "We were headed back from picking up our daughter at the airport when all this happened. Our car broke down a few miles back and started smoking and eventually caught on fire. Luckily we were all outside the vehicle when it burst into flames."

"Well come on and get in," Vince said, motioning with his hand. "We'll give you a ride."

They didn't waste any time and climbed onto the rear bench seat.

Cy reached back to move his bag off the seat as they got in. "Just throw that in the back."

"This is my son, Cy. We're coming from the airport ourselves," Vince said as they got into the wagon one by one. The big yellow Labrador Retriever hopped into the car after Reese and stuck his head over the front seat to greet Vince and Cy. Panting heavily, the dog gave the two a good sniff before Reese pulled him back by his collar.

"Sorry about that. Buster is a little hyper," Reese said, coaxing him into the back cargo area of the wagon.

"Good to see you, Cy," Fred said. "You probably don't remember us. You were just a kid when you and your mom moved away. This is my wife, Hannah, and our daughter, Reese. We've heard lots about you." Fred offered his hand as he got in and closed the door. Cy shook his hand and nodded at Hannah and Reese.

"Nice to meet you."

Fred looked at Vince. "Any idea what in the world is going on?"

"World War Three from the looks of it." Vince put the wagon in gear once everyone was in and settled. He accelerated quickly, leaving a cloud of dust behind them.

Hannah held her head in her hands. "I can't believe it. We barely made it out of the airport."

"We just made it out ourselves. The planes are dropping like flies," Cy said.

Vince sighed. "You kids are both very lucky that you had early flights."

"Yeah, we saw a few come down as we were getting out of there." Reese rubbed at her face, trying to hide her tears. They all looked like they had been through hell this morning, which made Vince appreciate his and Cy's luck and the old wagon even more.

"I guess these are EMPs, the way everything stopped working," Fred stammered. "We had the radio on before they hit. We heard the beginning of an emergency broadcast but then everything shorted out and the car died. Smoke started coming out of the vents a few seconds later, and before I could even bring the car to a complete stop, there were flames coming out from the edges of the hood. Thank goodness we got out when we did. It went up so fast. There were other cars around us that weren't as fortunate. There were some pretty bad accidents. A lot of people lost control of their cars. It all happened so fast."

"The electromagnetic pulse from the nukes has shut everything down and caused an overload. Anything electronic or controlled by a computer is toast." Vince slowed down as he navigated around a large truck and trailer that had jackknifed and blocked off most of the westbound lanes. The cab and the trailer were engulfed in flames, and even though he gave the burning wreck a wide berth as they passed, he could feel the heat from the fire. The charred remains of the driver, hunched over and hanging onto the wheel, was still visible. Vince tried not to look at the grotesque scene but couldn't help himself. The smell of burnt rubber and fuel filled his nostrils and stung the back of his throat with every breath.

No one said anything as they passed; they only

stared at what was becoming an all too familiar sight.

Hannah broke the silence. "What do you think it looks like back home?"

"I'm not sure, but from the looks of things, it's probably not good," Vince replied as he picked up speed again, eager to put the wreckage behind them.

What would they find in Cloverdale? Everyone in the car was probably thinking the same thing. If the pulse had caused this much damage to random vehicles and their electrical systems, what else had it done? What about houses and businesses connected to the electrical grid? Had they been hit by a surge of electricity as well? The results could be potentially catastrophic. Cloverdale hadn't been hit directly, but being only forty miles or so from Indianapolis, it wouldn't escape the blast or the effects of the electromagnetic pulse unscathed.

As Vince scanned the horizon and counted the tall black columns of smoke rising into the sky, he knew that no place would be immune. He didn't know what to expect when they got home, but it wouldn't be good.

· 8 ·

The interstate was a maze of wrecks and burning vehicles. Vince thought about how fortunate they were that it had happened on a Sunday and at such an early hour. Had it been a weekday during the morning commute, they probably wouldn't have been able to make their way back at all. As it was, the road was a challenge to navigate and the going was slow. Vince was getting impatient.

All he could think about were his friends and the shop and his house back in Cloverdale. Had they survived or suffered the same fate as some of the houses and businesses they passed along the interstate? He'd lost track of the number of buildings that were on fire, and those were only the ones they could see. The rising smoke suggested there were many more out of sight.

The air had become thick with a yellowish haze, casting a very unnatural tint over the landscape.

The temperature seemed to be rising faster than normal as well. He glanced at his watch and was surprised to see that his old Timex automatic still worked. At just a little after seven in the morning, it was already hotter than it should have been at this time of day. He wondered if the nukes had any effect on the atmosphere. It was possible and certainly would explain the heat. Over the last few months, he'd educated himself about the effects of a nuclear blast and knew a lot of it came down to the tonnage of the bomb and the altitude at which the detonation occurred.

Vince hoped Cloverdale would be safe from any nuclear fallout, providing the weather didn't exaggerate the effects of the blast. But Indianapolis as well as any other place that had been ground zero for a detonation would be a hot zone for months, possibly years, depending on all the different factors.

By the looks of the buildings in Indianapolis—or what was left of them—he assumed the detonation was somewhere between a high-altitude detonation and a ground-level burst. Was that the intended design or had the bomb malfunctioned? Whatever the case, the radiation it generated wouldn't reach out as fast as the blast force and thermal activity. At least that was what he hoped; otherwise, they were all doomed. They would know for sure in a couple days or hours, depending on the radiation levels they had been exposed to. High doses of radiation absorbed by the body could cause a myriad of health problems.

Most radiation passed through the human body, but tissue and organs absorbed a small amount. Anything over two hundred rem or rad—Vince never could figure out the difference—would cause sickness within a few hours. Anything over that, and the results would be grim.

No one had any rashes or reddening of the skin, so he was fairly confident that their exposure so far was low. There was always the possibility of health issues down the road, but that was of little concern to him now, and he couldn't think beyond the near future and getting home.

Vince glanced at the passengers in the back seat, then at Cy. "Everybody feeling okay?" he asked.

"Yeah, why?" Cy had a puzzled look on his face.

"I'm just concerned about radiation poisoning. I think we're okay, but if you feel nauseous or get a headache, let me know."

"And if we do?" Cy asked.

"If you do, we need to find some potassium iodine tablets," Reese interjected.

Cy turned to look at his newly found cousin.

Reese shrugged. "The thyroid gland is very sensitive to radiation. The tablets help prevent absorption into the gland. But it's only effective against radioactive iodine and isn't a cure-all."

"How do you know all this?" Cy asked.

"I'm studying to become a veterinarian at Cornell. Well, at least I was. I guess all that is over now." Reese turned away and hid her face as she looked out the window. Buster leaned over the seat and rested his head on her shoulder. She reached back and rubbed his head without turning around.

"Maybe it's not that bad," Cy said. "Maybe it's only like this in a few places. We can't be sure the whole country looks like this."

Vince wanted to believe there was some truth to what Cy was saying, but his gut told him otherwise. He saw the plumes rising across the horizon, and they all heard the distant rumblings of multiple detonations. There was no reason to believe that this horror hadn't played out all across the nation. To what extent it had, they might never know.

With communications and emergency services down, there was no telling when or if help would ever come to them or anyone. At this point, the government was surely in self-preservation mode. For all Vince knew, there was no government anymore. If the North Koreans were behind this, Washington D.C. would be a high-priority target, and so would most major military bases around the country. If a relatively unimportant place like Indianapolis was a target, then it was reasonable to assume there were a high number of detonations.

In the grand scheme of things, Indianapolis had little strategic military value. If enough ICBMs were launched that Indianapolis became a target, then all bets were off and the entire country was probably in chaos.

For the time being, they needed to accept the fact that they were on their own. Vince decided then and there that the first priority when they got back to Cloverdale was to grab any able-bodied person he could find and form a rescue party. They'd go house to house and building to building until they covered the town. There was strength in numbers, and they would need all the help they could get.

Not only would they need to gather survivors, but they also needed to start gathering and stockpiling supplies. They could be on their own for God knows how long—months, maybe years. Would they ever see normalcy again? He doubted it, but he held out hope that someday Cy and Reese would have a normal life or semblance of one. And it was up to him to make that happen. This was about survival; this was about making sure there was a future for them in this apocalyptic world.

. 9 .

As Vince approached the exit for Cloverdale, he saw dark clouds of smoke hanging over the town, and his heart sank. Multiple columns of thick gray smoke rose from everywhere, it seemed. There were too many fires to count as he made the turn and exited the interstate. Time stood still for a moment while he strained to see through the thick haze. Had his garage survived the pulse? To say Vince was relieved to see the garage intact was an understatement, and he headed straight for it.

His joy was short-lived, though. The amount of damage was staggering. He could count on one hand the number of buildings and houses that survived the EMP blast. Among them were the motel across the street and a few small vacant homes at the beginning of the residential section.

There was no movement otherwise—not a soul in sight. Besides his shop, the next closest gas station was completely engulfed in flames that had long ago blown the pumps. The skeleton of a delivery truck was partially exposed and sticking out the side of the building. Its side panels had melted away, leaving only the rugged steel frame.

As Vince pulled into the parking area of his shop, he searched for Bill's truck but failed to find it anywhere. He wasn't surprised and assumed Bill had run back home when it all happened. His older-model Dodge pickup should have survived the pulse. He hoped Bill had made it home in time to save Sarah and their little girl Sasha.

When Vince got out of the car, the first thing he noticed was the large plate-glass windows in the storefront. They each had several long cracks running from one side of their frames to the other. The only thing holding them together was the tinted glazing that helped keep the sun out.

No one said a word as they hopped out of the car and looked around, The damage was overwhelming. In a matter of hours, their once sleepy little town had been transformed into a fiery wasteland. The air was thick with floating debris and smoke, making it difficult to draw a full breath without gagging or choking.

"Come on. Follow me," Vince ordered. He led them into the shop and ran behind the counter. He searched the lower shelf and pulled out a handful of paper filter masks. He'd bought a pack a while ago while doing some insulation work at the shop.

At the time, he complained about having to buy a twelve-pack when he only needed one. Now he was glad he had enough to go around.

"Here, put these on. We shouldn't be breathing this stuff in." Vince took one and threw the pack to Cy, who took one and handed the rest to Reese. She took one and tried to fasten it over Buster's face, but he wasn't having it. He pawed at the mask and knocked it off quickly.

"Just worry about yourself. He's down low enough to the ground that I think he'll be all right," Vince said.

Once they all had their masks on, they stood around for a moment and looked at each other in disbelief. The relative calm inside the storefront made it hard to accept what was going on outside. There was a part of Vince that wanted to stay put.

Vince realized that he was going to have to take charge of the situation. As he looked at the mask-covered faces of the people around him, he could see the shock and unwillingness to accept what was going on in their eyes.

Hannah adjusted her mask. "What do we do?"

"We look for survivors. I have a couple cars out back in the yard that I think might still run. Wait here while I look for the keys," Vince ordered.

In his mind, he ran through the inventory of cars at the shop. What did they have that was drivable? There was an older Chevy van that had a bad transmission. It would run but only had a few gears that worked. It still beat walking and would hold a lot of people or supplies. He looked through the cabinet where they kept the keys for all the vehicles they currently had at the shop. He found the van keys and also the keys to an old Toyota pickup that had come in for muffler work. He headed back out to the storefront and found everyone standing around in silence. The only movement came from Buster, who had wandered off to the snack section and was sniffing the candy bars.

Vince tossed the van keys to Fred. "There's a black Chevy van out back. It's only got a couple gears, but she'll run."

"Okay." Fred stood motionless for a moment before he snapped to. "Okay, we'll start looking for people."

"You'll have to go out the front and around. The back door isn't working. Oh, and if you come across anything useful, don't hesitate to grab it. Food, clothing, weapons, whatever you can find," Vince added.

"Weapons?" Fred made a face.

Vince nodded. "That's right. I don't see things staying civil for too long."

"You really think it will come to that?" Reese asked.

"Let's hope not, but we need to be prepared to defend what we have," Vince answered. The truth was, Vince had little hope for avoiding conflict and was sure that, sooner or later, it would come down to their ability to protect themselves and their supplies. He knew there were people out there who would seek to capitalize on the catastrophe. Someone tried to break into his shop last night, after all, and that was under normal circumstances. With no law enforcement, it would be up to them to protect what they had, and the more prepared they were, the better off they would be.

"We can start taking survivors to the motel across the street," Vince said, eager to change the subject. He handed the other set of keys to Cy and looked at his son.

"You up for this on your own?"

Cy took a step forward and grabbed the keys. "I got it, Dad."

"Buster and I can go with you," Reese offered.

"Honey, no. I want you with your mother and me," Fred pleaded.

"Dad, it's okay. There's no point in all of us going together. We can get more done in teams," Reese shot back.

Vince was impressed with her willingness to step up and was glad to see her volunteer without hesitation. It also made him feel better to know that Cy wouldn't be alone in case he ran into trouble.

Cy looked at his dad. "What about you?"

"I'll be fine. Everybody be careful. Don't take

any unnecessary risks and don't waste time trying to put out any fires. People and supplies are the priority."

They all nodded in agreement and headed out into the parking lot. As soon as Vince stepped outside, he could feel the heat from the fires and a sting in the back of his throat from the soot in the air. The mask helped a little but was never meant for this type of use. It filtered out airborne particles but did nothing to block the pungent burnt odor that permeated the air and was a harsh reminder that their town was dying.

As the others made their way to the back lot, he locked the door to the shop out of habit and headed for the wagon. There was no time to waste as he thought about the events of the morning and where Mary might have been when it all happened. He fired the engine up and threw the car into gear. He began to pull out of the lot when he suddenly stopped.

He should wait and make sure the others could start their vehicles and get on their way. He sat and watched the gate impatiently. The blue Toyota pickup pulled through the opening first. Cy drove and Reese rode shotgun while Buster sat on the seat between them.

Cy gave him a thumbs-up as he pulled out slowly and headed down Main Street. The Toyota quickly disappeared from sight and into the drifting smoke. The van appeared next as Fred nursed it along and out of the lot. It was in bad shape, but Vince hoped it would hold out long enough to be of some use. What choice did they have? All the other cars at the garage were either newer models and wouldn't start or didn't even run at all.

The van pulled out and headed in the same direction Cy and Reese had gone. Vince worried about his son, but there was no time for that now. Every minute mattered and might be the difference between life and death for those people fortunate enough to avoid being trapped in their homes and burned alive.

· 10 ·

Cy leaned forward as he drove the old Toyota into the swirling clouds of smoke. There were moments when he could only see a few feet in front of the truck. It cleared up for brief periods and allowed them to see a little farther at times, but as they approached the residential area of town, the smoke enveloped them once more. As they passed the burning houses, he began to wonder if they would find any survivors. Most of the homes they passed were already consumed by flames, and the rest were well on their way. If there were people inside, they were long gone. He did his best to keep the truck in the center of the street. Too close to one side or the other and the heat from the fires was almost unbearable.

The situation seemed hopeless, but when he was about to say something to Reese, he spotted something through the haze.

It was a couple walking on the road. He slammed on the brakes to avoid running them over. Buster slid into the dashboard and quickly climbed back onto the seat, letting out a few nervous whimpers.

The couple looked shocked to see a pickup heading toward them and froze in their tracks. Covered in soot and coughing, they carried a small child who looked unconscious or, worse, dead. The woman's face had two clean streaks under each eye, where tears had washed the soot away.

Cy threw the truck into neutral and put on the emergency brake before he hopped out. He didn't dare turn it off. Back in the yard, the truck had been reluctant to start at all, and he didn't want to get stuck here.

"Come on. Get in the back. We'll get you out of here," Cy called out.

The couple stood motionless for a moment before they reacted and started for the truck. "What's happening?" the man asked, coughing through a rag that he held over his nose and mouth.

"We're under attack. Nukes." Cy could barely believe the words as they came out of his mouth. Next to him, Reese appeared out of nowhere and didn't waste any time escorting the woman to the back of the truck and into the bed. The man followed, handing the boy to his wife before climbing in next. The child moved a little on his own and then coughed. Before now, Cy hadn't been sure if the boy was alive or not.

The man coughed again. "Where are you taking us?"

"The old motel in town. You'll be safe there." Cy nodded and closed the tailgate. He wasn't sure if they would be safe at the motel or not, but that was what his dad had said to do. Besides, by the looks of things, there wasn't anywhere else to go.

This was no time for introductions, and Cy and Reese hurried back into the truck, where Buster waited impatiently and greeted them with excited sniffing and panting as he bounced back and forth across the bench seat. Cy considered how lucky the dog was to be oblivious to what was going on around them. Finally, with some coaxing from Reese, Buster settled into his spot between them like he'd been riding there his whole life.

"We need to get them out of the smoke, and they all need oxygen, especially the boy." Reese rubbed Buster's head and tried to settle him down.

"Where do we get that?" Cy asked.

"Head for the fire department. They should have what we need."

"I'm not sure how to get there," Cy said with a shrug. "Do you want to drive?"

Reese glanced down at the manual shifter. "I don't know how to drive this thing, but I'll give you directions. Just head back the way we came for now."

Cy nodded and did a tidy three-point turn on the road, thankful they weren't going any farther into the chaos, at least not for the time being. Reese directed him through a few turns, and eventually they ended up at the firehouse—or what was left of it. Cy was disappointed but not surprised to find the building in ruins. For the most part, the concrete walls still stood, but the wooden trussed roof had caved in and was a burning heap of embers atop the still-parked emergency vehicles, making them inaccessible. Cy wondered what had become of the fireman. Were their bodies buried in the rubble? Both he and Reese stared for a minute and contemplated their next move. Maybe they should just drive back to the motel. It was getting worse by the minute out here and harder to see. There were people in the back of the truck now that were exposed and already in bad shape.

He looked at Reese. "Now what?"

"We really need to find oxygen for the boy. Let's try the pharmacy—if it's still there," Reese said with a sigh.

"Just point the way."

After a few more turns and what seemed like hours at such a slow speed, they arrived at a slightly intact drug store. The building was on fire, but not as badly as some of the other places they had seen. Cy was about to suggest they let it go, but Reese had other plans.

"Come on. Let's see what we can salvage." She was already halfway out of the truck before Cy could argue with her. He shifted into neutral and killed the engine, letting the Toyota drift the last couple of inches until it came to an abrupt stop against the curb in front of the drug store.

"We need to try to find oxygen for your son and anything else we can save that might be useful," Reese shouted back to the couple in the truck bed. The mother was still holding the boy closely and didn't bother looking up.

"I'll help." The man huffed as he climbed over the side the truck and joined them.

"You sure you're okay to help?" Cy asked.

"I'll be fine," he said through a cough.

Cy nodded and the three of them approached what was left of the building. The left half of the drug store was a total loss. Several large fires raged, so salvaging anything from that part of the store was impossible. The windows had been blown out across the front, and they decided to climb in through one of the large openings on the opposite side.

"Watch for glass!" Reese cautioned as she gingerly made her way over the jagged shards still embedded in the window frame. Cy offered his hand for balance as she high-stepped through the window and into the storefront. The shattered bits of glass crackled under their feet until they were well inside. The smoke was filling the place quickly and formed a dense white cloud that extended a few feet down from the ceiling. They had to crouch down as they pushed farther in. Cy's dad probably wouldn't approve of this, but Reese was right: if they didn't get what they could now, it would all be lost.

"Grab whatever you can," Reese said. "Water, bandages, anything to treat burns. I'll look around behind the counter for any meds we might need."

Cy spotted a section of shelving that had bandages and ointments and began loading them into a small hand basket he'd grabbed near the front of the store. The man followed his lead and did the same. Every time they finished loading a basket, they would carry it to the front and place it outside the broken window, then grab another and go back for more.

"Cy, back here. Bring a basket!" Reese yelled from somewhere in the back. He grabbed an empty basket and headed toward the sound of her voice. As he made his way behind the pharmacist counter, he saw a pile of supplies on the floor, including a few small oxygen bottles complete with masks and tubing. Reese, her arms full of bottles and boxes, appeared from behind a large shelving unit. She headed right for him and unloaded them into the basket he was holding.

"We need to take what we have and get out of here. There're a lot more oxygen tanks locked up in the back that I can't get to and the fire is getting close. We don't have long before this place blows!" Reese glanced at Cy with a frantic look on her face, then started gathering the pile of supplies on the floor and stuffing them into a bag she'd found. He helped her get the rest of it into his basket, and they headed for the front of the store.

"We need to go, now!" Cy shouted to the man, who was still loading supplies from the shelves. He stopped and looked at them as they passed. He grabbed what he could carry and followed. Once outside, they dragged everything away from the store and ran it to the truck in several trips, hastily throwing it all into the back.

"Careful with that one," Reese cautioned. Cy could hear glass bottles clinking together as he loaded the last bag Reese handed to him. The man rejoined his wife and son in the back of the truck and sat down among the mess of supplies.

Cy hurried into the driver's seat and started the truck. About to throw it in gear and back out, he realized Reese hadn't joined him yet. He looked back through the window and saw her strapping a mask over the boy's face and giving some quick instructions to the mother.

"Let's go!" he shouted. Glancing at the pharmacy from the outside, he couldn't believe how much the fire had spread since they arrived. The flames were now leaping through the roof and some of the side windows.

Reese hurried to the passenger's seat and pushed Buster back as she jumped in and slammed the door behind her.

"Go!" she shouted.

Cy threw the truck in reverse and the rear wheels chirped as he backed away from the curb. He cut the wheel hard and maneuvered the truck backward down the street until he swung the front end around. He put the truck in first gear and spun the tires again, then popped the clutch. They lurched forward, and he looked back to make sure his passengers were okay. He hadn't meant to do that, but it had been a while since he drove a stick and he was rushing. He was about to apologize for his driving when an explosion rang out. Several more followed and they looked back to see a large fireball rising up from the drug store.

Cy looked at Reese. "That was close."

"But it was worth it," she said and pointed to the boy and his mother in the back. The boy had his eyes open now and was holding the oxygen mask to his face on his own. Teary-eyed, the father turned to face Cy and Reese and nodded as he mouthed the words "thank you."

· 11 ·

Vince had broken off from the others and headed in the opposite direction. He would check the hardware store first, then Mary's house. It went against his instincts and better judgment to let the kids go off on their own, but there was little choice in the matter if they were going to cover a lot of ground quickly.

At the rate these fires were burning, before long there would be nothing left of the town. Without emergency services available, there would be no help, no firefighters to put out the countless fires, and no medical aid for those unfortunate enough to be injured. Even if these services were still available, the current need far outweighed the resources of a small town like Cloverdale.

He briefly considered going to his house first to see if anything was left, but he decided to put it off. Mary's house was on the way, and that was far more important to him right now. Once he got to

Mary, they could make their way out to his place to see if his house was still standing.

Even if it was burnt to the ground, all might not be lost. He kept his gun safe in the basement, and it was a good-quality sixty long-gun-capacity fire-rated safe. It cost him a small fortune, and he had done his research. If he was going to pay that kind of money for something, he was going to get the best. The one he chose had a 120-minute fire rating and was supposed to withstand temperatures of up to two thousand degrees. Another feature the company boasted about and seemed like a waste of money at the time was the EMP-proof high-security digital keypad and bypass key. Even if the keypad was destroyed or melted, the bypass key he had on his keychain would open the door.

The safe was bigger than he needed, but he liked the idea of being able to keep other things in there along with his firearms, so after much research, he went for it and bought the biggest model. The thing weighed 1,250 pounds and took him and Bill and a healthy dose of trust in the old wooden steps to get the safe down into the basement. But they managed to wrestle it into place over a couple beers one Saturday evening, and now it was all worth it. And because of the extra room in the safe, he was able to keep a decent amount of canned goods along with a case of MREs that he took on all-day hunting trips. He also had a few valuables in the safe and the deed to the property. But most importantly, he had his hunting rifles and a couple shotguns, along with a fair amount of ammo for all of them, including the .45 still tucked under his seat. Among the guns in the safe was one of his favorites: a Springfield Armory M1A-A1 semi-automatic Scout squad rifle chambered in .308. He used the gun for deer hunting occasionally but mostly for target-shooting. He ran the gun with iron sights and loved the simplicity of it. He had a steel plate set up at one hundred yards behind the house and could drain the twenty-round magazine in less than thirty seconds with every round finding the target.

The safe would be there, fire or no fire, and he'd find out if the money he paid for it was worth it after all. But right now, every minute wasted could be the difference between life and death for Mary. His top priority was finding her and anyone else that was fortunate enough to survive this.

He adjusted his grip on the steering wheel nervously. It was frustrating not being able to drive faster, but the thick smoke made it nearly impossible to see more than twenty or thirty yards in front of the car.

As he rounded the corner, he saw that the hardware store had been reduced to a pile of burning rubble, and his heart sank in his chest. Fortunately, he didn't see Mary's white Jeep where she normally parked out front.

Disappointed to see the store in ruins but unwilling to accept defeat, Vince wasted no time in turning the car south and heading to Mary's house. She was an early riser, and with any luck, today was no exception. She was fortunate enough to have one of the larger properties in town, right on the edge of the residential area. She was a self-sufficient woman and took great pride in that, one of her many qualities Vince admired.

On her small farmette she raised chickens and goats along with a few ducks. Last time they talked, she admitted that it was getting out of hand and that she had over a dozen chickens, a handful of goats, and a few pigs roaming the yard. It wasn't this way by design, but she had a hard time saying no and had rescued a few critters over the years.

She always had more eggs than she could use. With most of the birds laying an egg a day, they piled up quickly. At least once a week, she brought a basketful for him to use or give away along with his produce, although he always kept the larger duck eggs for himself, as they were his favorite.

Vince made the left onto Lincoln Avenue and followed it away from North Main Street. There were only a handful of houses on this road, and the air quality, along with his visibility, began to improve a little as he followed the road farther away from town. Vince held his breath as he passed the first home and was disappointed to see that it had not been spared the effects of the EMPs. The fire had already reached the second floor as flames poured out of the second-story windows and curled upward toward the roof.

Mary's house wasn't far now, just around the next turn. He leaned forward over the steering wheel and strained to find her house through the thinning smoke. He was pleasantly surprised to see the old yellow two-story farmhouse still standing and seemingly unaffected. He felt a small amount of relief as he turned into the gravel drive and sped to the house, leaving a cloud of dust behind the wagon. As he parked and turned the car off, the familiar sound of chickens clucking greeted him. Her one lone rooster ran over to inspect him as Vince stepped out of the car, but the bird got sidetracked by his reflection in one of the polished chrome hubcaps.

Vince paused for a moment and surveyed his surroundings. Other than the occasional cloud of smoke that drifted across the property and the lingering burnt odor that seemed to cling to everything, he'd never know he was in the middle of World War Three. But he was, and a quick scan of the horizon and the rising black plumes of ash brought him back to reality.

Vince was concerned that there was no sign of Mary anywhere. Any other time he'd stopped by, she would be out on the front porch, waiting to greet him. He jogged up the steps to the front door and knocked. It was louder than he meant to knock, and he hoped he hadn't scared her. Mary had a shotgun and knew how to use it. In light of the day's events, she probably had it handy.

Vince was relieved to see Nugget, Mary's Blue Heeler, run to the door and bark at him through the sidelight. Nugget went everywhere with her, and it gave Vince hope that Mary wasn't far behind. Sure enough, he spotted her coming to the door. She approached cautiously, probably because of the way he knocked, and he immediately felt bad for causing her alarm.

"It's me, Vince," he called through the frosted glass sidelight. "Are you okay?"

He could see her distorted outline through the glass as she approached the door. It slowly opened until Nugget had enough room to slip out.

"Oh, thank God. It's you, Vince!" She surprised him with a hug and pulled him inside. "Nugget, get your butt in here!" she scolded. The little dog had taken the opportunity to wander onto the porch and was already halfway down the steps. She sniffed at the air, holding her nose up as high as she could before reluctantly heeding Mary's call to come back inside. Mary closed the door behind her as she sauntered into the house.

Her eyes widened. "What's going on? Are these nuclear bombs?"

Vince followed her into the kitchen, where she glanced through the window that looked out over her back yard and the wheat fields beyond. From there, he could see several black plumes of smoke rising on the distant horizon.

"Yes, I think so. EMPs actually."

"I was out feeding the animals and collecting eggs when it happened. Nugget and I came inside right away and haven't been back outside since. I wasn't sure what to do. I've been trying to get the news on that little hand-held radio but nothing's coming in." Mary pointed to a small black and yellow hand-cranked emergency radio on the kitchen table next to the morning's collection of eggs.

"It's bad out there. Really bad. There's no power anywhere and…and the town is… Well, the town is on fire, at least most of it. I was in Indianapolis picking Cy up from the airport. We're lucky to be alive." Vince shook his head. "The hardware store is gone."

"What? What do you mean *gone*?" She sat down at the kitchen table.

Vince pulled out a chair, sat down next to her, and put his hand on her knee. "Burned to the ground. Most places are. There isn't much left, or at least there won't be by morning. I was surprised to find your house still standing. You're lucky! We all are."

"I don't feel very lucky right now." Mary took her hands away from her face and looked at Vince as if she suddenly felt guilty for her comment.

"Is Cy all right?" she asked.

Vince nodded. "Yeah, he's fine. But we got out of there just in time. Indianapolis is in ruins, and from the looks of things, it's not the only place. The nukes caused a power surge, and from what I can tell, they wiped out all things electronic. There isn't much left out there that works anymore. We ran into the Morgans on the way back from Indy. They were picking up their daughter Reese at the airport when their car caught on fire. We found them walking on the side of the road and brought them back to town with us."

Nugget wandered over and lay down at the base of Mary's chair. Staring at the radio on the table, Mary reached down and scratched Nugget's head briefly. "How could all this happen? I don't understand."

"I don't have any answers, but I do know that we need to act fast and save what we can. What do you say? Are you up to riding with me and looking for survivors and supplies?"

The expression on Mary's face changed and she sat up in her chair.

"Okay."

· 12 ·

Mary gathered a few bottles of water from her still-cold refrigerator and grabbed a pair of work gloves on their way out the door. With Nugget close behind, they made their way onto the porch. Vince smelled what was now a familiar odor, and it reminded him of the extra masks he had in the car.

"Better lock it up," he cautioned.

"You really think so?" Mary asked.

"I'm afraid so. Someone tried to break into the shop last night. Can't be too safe. From what I've seen, you've got one of the few places still standing, which means it's likely to attract some unwanted guests."

Mary shook her head as she locked the deadbolt on the door. Vince thought about telling her to grab her shotgun, but he didn't want her to panic. They could come back and get it later, along with some of her things. He didn't want her staying out here alone. Not now. It wouldn't be safe. She wouldn't be happy about it and would probably argue the point, but Vince would hold his ground on this and insist she stay with them in town. They could figure out what to do with the animals sometime down the road.

"It's a shame about the break-ins around town. I guess it's not going to get any better now, is it?" she said.

"No, I guess not. In fact, I imagine things are about to get a lot worse. Once people start to run out of food and water, they'll get pretty desperate. That's why I've been thinking about pooling our resources and making a stand in town. The old motel across the street from my garage is still standing. With a little work, I could supply the place with power and probably work out a way to get running water too."

"How long do you think we'll be without electric and other services?" Mary asked.

Vince realized she hadn't grasped the gravity of the situation yet. Vince took a deep breath and looked at Mary. "It's going to be a while."

Truth was, it was going to be more than a while. Depending on the targets and the accuracy of the ICBMs aimed at those targets, it could potentially be years. He hoped he was wrong, but his gut told him otherwise.

She hadn't seen the devastation and destruction he had. But soon enough, she would. This was an isolated little pocket outside of town—a welcome sight after what he'd seen today—but it wasn't reality anymore. Life seemed so complicated all of a sudden. Or was it simpler now? He couldn't decide. Either way, it would never be the same again; that was for sure.

His mind was going in a million different directions at once. He wasn't just trying to process what was happening; he was beginning to come up with a plan and ideas for their survival. He was as shocked as everyone else when the first bomb went off, but he also knew and accepted that they were on their own.

Nugget was already at the wagon, sniffing around the tires, when Vince and Mary reached the car. She wasted no time getting in and taking a spot on the front bench seat, where she sat upright with a good view out the front window. It wasn't Nugget's first time in Vince's car. He and Mary often went for drives through the countryside on lazy Sunday evenings. They usually ended up at the Chocolate Moose down in Bloomington for an ice cream and a hot dog for Nugget. If the weather was nice, they'd put the windows down and let Nugget hang out in the wind, tongue dangling from the side of her mouth, tail wagging. The dog liked that part, even more than having a whole hotdog to herself.

Vince didn't mind the little dog and had in fact

grown fond of her over the years. She was an energetic little thing and sometimes moved about so fast it was comical. He got a kick out of watching her chase the chickens around the yard when they wandered too close to her outdoor water bowl.

But they wouldn't have the windows down on their drive today. And there'd be no more going to the Chocolate Moose on quiet Sunday evenings. This would most likely be the worst drive they would ever take together. Their town, the place they were born and raised, was dying before their eyes. And there wasn't much they could do about it other than try to save as many people as they could. On his way out to Mary's, though, Vince began to doubt they would find many survivors.

If power was lost and all things electronic were hit with a pulse of electricity strong enough to cause fires and melt wiring, then battery backed-up smoke alarms wouldn't be much use. He imagined a lot of folks never woke up this morning and never would again. It seemed that the majority of the houses and buildings in town were on fire. He wondered if the solar electric system he installed at the garage had saved it from a similar fate.

Vince educated himself on solar systems before he signed on the dotted line with an installation company. Indiana had some great incentive programs, and one of them was the net metering program, which allowed him to sell the extra electricity he generated with the rooftop panels back to the power company for credits in kilowatt hours.

This required the installation of a net meter with a master shut-off switch so any extra electricity he generated beyond what the storage batteries could hold went back to the grid. The cut-off switch had an inline circuit breaker between it, and the inverter was specifically designed to protect against a surge of power in either direction. That was probably what saved his shop. In fact, Mary had solar panels on her barn out back, and they might have saved her house too.

If the circuit breaker had done its job—and he assumed it did, since both the garage and Mary's house were still standing—then the inverter must have been protected as well. The inverter changed the DC current from the panels on the roof to usable AC current. If that was the case, then it should be fairly easy to turn the power back on at both places. At least, that was what he was counting on. But power was far from being a priority. Right now, they had people to save and supplies to gather—if they were lucky enough to find either.

· 13 ·

As Cy and Reese approached the motel, Cy noticed an old Jeep in the parking lot. He didn't remember seeing it parked there when they were across the street at his dad's shop, but it would have been easy to miss in the chaos. He pulled in slowly and parked by the front office and check-in desk.

"I'll go try and find a room key. Why don't you check on them and see if the boy is all right? We can get them set up in one of the rooms and head back out." Cy turned the truck off as he looked back at their passengers. They needed to get the boy inside and out of the smoke, but he wasn't sure about the heading back out part.

"Sounds good. Looks like he's doing better. I wasn't even sure he was alive when we first found them," Reese said, glancing back.

"I know. Me neither." Cy rolled his eyes before he hopped out and headed toward the motel. He could hear Reese pleading with Buster to stay put as she got out of the truck to check on the boy and his parents.

He looked over at the first red door to the right of the front office: room 101. He assumed the keys would be easy to find and figured he'd grab the one for the closest room to the truck. No point in carrying the supplies any farther than they had to. Should they keep the stuff they had gathered here? Or maybe it might be better to take it over to his dad's garage. He already had an uneasy feeling about waltzing into a strange motel and helping himself to room keys.

As he entered the office, he looked around and made his way behind the counter. There was a small office just beyond the counter, and inside was a board with a row of room keys dangling neatly. He darted to the board and grabbed the oversized plastic tag with "101" on it. He paused for a second, then grabbed the key for room 102. They could put the stuff there for now and move it later if his dad wanted.

"Hold it right there." Cy froze in his tracks and did as the stern voice behind him ordered. "Get your hands up where I can see them!" the voice continued. He complied and raised his hands without turning around.

"What are you doing in here?" the voice asked.

Cy turned to face the shiny silver barrel of a large

revolver pointed directly at him. He could see into the open-ended cylinders of the gun and noticed the hollowed-out tips of each bullet. The gun was definitely loaded, and this was really happening. The man holding the gun looked to be about his dad's age and wore a camouflage baseball cap. From the look on his face, Cy guessed that he wasn't fooling around or afraid to use the gun.

"I... I'm Vince Walker's son, Cy. We have some people that need medical attention. My dad said to use the motel."

Just then, Reese came in and startled the man. He nervously spun around and pointed the gun in her direction, then back at Cy. He backpedaled to the other side of the room so he could keep an eye on them both. He juggled the gun back and forth, keeping it trained on them as best as he could.

"Get over there with him. Both of you, keep your hands where I can see them," he barked.

Reese joined Cy by the front desk, keeping her hands up as she moved. "We're not here to cause any trouble. We have a family out there in need of help. We were just going to use a room here temporarily. We're with the Major," she pleaded.

"And what makes you think you can do that, huh?" the man snarled.

This wasn't going well, and the man seemed to be getting more agitated every time they tried to explain their situation. Cy wished his dad would hurry up and get back. They could really use some help right about now.

"Are you part of the gang that's been breaking into people places around town lately?" The man pointed with the gun as he talked.

"No, we don't know anything about that. I told you I'm Vince Walker's son. This is Reese Morgan. Her parents live just outside town. My dad and her parents will be back any minute. It was their idea to use the motel for the time being. Why would we break into a motel with all this going on?" Cy looked out the window, then back at the man. He could tell the man didn't know what to do and was confused.

"Jim, what are you doing? Put the gun down before you hurt somebody." The man that Cy and Reese had picked up in town, along with the boy and mother, stormed into the office. He coughed as he spoke.

"But they were... I was..." The man stuttered as the expression on his face changed from anger to embarrassment. He slowly lowered the gun and looked down, clearly ashamed.

"Are you really the Major's boy?"

The gun hung limply at his side now, and before Cy could answer, the man spoke up again. "These two just saved my son's life. If it wasn't for them, well, I don't know." The man approached Reese and Cy and extended a hand in Cy's direction.

"I never really got to thank you two properly or introduce myself. I could hardly breathe when you guys found us, let alone talk. The name's Tom. My wife Beverly and I are forever grateful for what you did for us and our boy, Ryan. We're all lucky to be alive. We barely made it out of our house this morning."

Cy nodded and took Tom's hand. "No problem. Glad to be able to help."

Tom shook Reese's hand next, and Cy kept an eye on the man with the gun, who was now shuffling toward them. "I'm really sorry about that," Jim said and offered his hand as well. "I guess I'm a little on edge and got carried away."

"It's okay." Glancing at Reese, Cy took what felt like the first breath he'd taken since staring down the barrel of a loaded gun. Thank God Tom had come in when he had. There was no telling how this would have gone down without his interference.

Cy suddenly realized how tightly he was holding the room keys in his left hand and loosened his grip. They had dug into his palm, leaving a red key-shaped impression.

"We need to get your son into a room," Reese reminded everyone and took one of the keys from Cy. "We also need to unload the truck and get back out there to look for anything or anyone else we can save."

She was right. At the rate things were burning, they didn't have long before all was lost. If there were any others out there, they needed to find them — and fast.

The smoke was thicker than Cy remembered, and when they left the motel office, he repositioned the mask on his face, squeezing the wire around the nose piece to create a better seal. Outside room 101, Tom's wife and son sat with their backs against the building. The boy still had the oxygen mask on his face and was breathing heavily into it. His mother rubbed his shoulders with one hand and wiped at her soot-covered face with the other. She managed a crooked smile when she saw Cy coming toward them with the room key.

He pressed his shoulder into the door and pushed as he turned the key. The stubborn red door gave way with a groan, and he stepped into a motel room straight out of the '70s. Reese and Tom helped the boy and his mother inside and led them over to the bed. They got the boy situated and propped him up on his side with a couple pillows while Cy headed back out to unload what they gathered from the drug store.

Jim followed him out to the Toyota, and Cy threw him the key to room 102.

"Let's put these supplies in the next room over for now." Jim opened up the room before rejoining Cy at the back of the truck.

Buster steamed up the windows inside the Toyota with his hot breath as he bounded from window to window in excitement. Reese and Tom joined them shortly and helped with the last few baskets of supplies.

"Does the Jeep run?" Cy asked.

Jim nodded. "It does."

"Good. Why don't you and Tom follow us back into town and help us look for people and supplies? You up for that?" Cy looked at Tom, who launched into another fit of coughing while carrying the last basket to the room.

Tom cleared his throat. "Yeah, I'll be fine."

"All right then. Let's get going," Cy said.

"We'll be right behind you. Let me tell my wife where we're going."

"Good, she can stay here and let the others know where we are when they get here," Reese added.

Tom nodded in agreement and headed for the room.

"All right. Let's do this." Cy opened the driver's door and was greeted by an overly excited Buster. The whole truck smelled like dog, even through the mask. It was the first time Cy noticed a smell other than smoke. Buster jumped to the other side as Reese got in, whipping Cy in the face with his tail as it wagged.

"Sorry about that," she said, shaking her head.

"He has no idea what's going on."

"He's lucky." Cy started the truck and began backing up as Buster settled into the middle of the seat and leaned into him.

He flicked the headlights on, though he wasn't sure why he bothered. The lights made little difference in terms of visibility, but it was all they had. At the very least, maybe they would let others see them on the road. The last thing they needed was to get into an accident. He waited at the exit from the motel parking lot until Jim and Tom were behind them in the Jeep. Creeping out onto the street, he turned toward town and headed into the dark gray wall of smoke that drifted across the road.

The motel soon faded from sight in the rearview mirror, and Cy hoped the others were okay. He shot Reese an uneasy look. He could hardly believe they were going back out into this, but what choice did they have?

· 14 ·

Vince and Mary headed north on Lincoln Avenue, back toward Main Street. On the front seat, Nugget sat patiently between them, sniffing loudly, occasionally getting more than she bargained for in the soot-laden air, and sneezing as a result. This reminded Vince of the extra masks he had, so he reached into the back seat and grabbed one for Mary.

"Here you go. Better put this on. It gets worse," Vince warned.

Mary took the mask and pulled the yellow strap over her head as she looked out the window. Squeezing the nose piece, she took a deep breath. "Thanks."

She glanced at him but quickly turned her attention back to the chaos outside the car. As they made their way closer to town, the air began to grow thicker with smoke. Soon, visibility was so poor that Vince had to slow down to a frustratingly slow speed.

Mary stared in silence at the burning houses as they drove. Vince kept his eyes on the road and turned his headlights on out of instinct. The lights didn't make any noticeable difference and only seemed to highlight the particles drifting through the air. It reminded him of driving through a heavy snowstorm.

"Wow, I can't believe this," Mary mumbled through the mask as she shook her head.

It was a lot to take in. House after house was on fire, and Vince realized that even if some of the homes had been spared initially, they would soon catch fire from the flames drifting over from their neighbors. There was nothing to stop it. The only places that would survive were those that had space around them and hadn't caught fire by themselves. He noticed a difference already, even though he came through this part of town not that long ago. The smoke was thicker and the fires larger.

At that moment, Vince thought about his good friend John and his deputies. They had been out and about early this morning. Surely they were still okay, out here in this mess somewhere, no doubt fighting their own battles. If their vehicles were running, they all probably went to help their families first, and who could blame them?

As Vince turned onto Main Street, they passed a large oak tree on the corner. It was completely engulfed in fire, no doubt caused by the flames jumping from the house next to it. To make matters worse, the wind was picking up. He couldn't tell if the fires or the weather caused it. There were small whirlwinds of fire rising up here and there, and for the first time since this started, Vince felt completely helpless. Maybe this was a foolish thing to be doing. Should they abandon looking for people and supplies and hunker down somewhere safe?

It was getting harder to breathe by the minute, and the cheap dust masks weren't up to the task. The burning in Vince's throat had gone from a minor irritation to a constant annoyance, and he decided then and there that they needed to get through town and find the kids. They were going to have to cut their losses and get out of this smoke. He felt guilty now for taking Mary from her house. She would have been better off there. If not for the others, he would have turned around and gone back.

"I don't think we should be out in this. I can take you back home," he said between coughs.

"Nonsense. Let's find the others first and then we can all go back to my house." Mary handed Vince one of the waters she brought from her house. He moved the mask to the side and took a drink. It helped his throat, but he knew it was only temporary. They couldn't keep this up for long. This rescue attempt was quickly turning into survival for them.

Vince felt Mary's fingernails dig into his arm before he saw the small herd of deer run across the road in front of them.

"Look out!" she yelled.

Vince slammed on the brakes just in time, narrowly avoiding one of them as they crossed. A large doe paused in front of the wagon and stared at them before resuming her sprint away from the flaming houses. Nugget regained her composure from the sudden stop and put her front paws on the dashboard. At the sight of the deer, she let out several sharp barks before Mary pulled her down onto the seat.

"Easy, girl. It's all right," Mary said, but the little dog barked a few more times.

Vince watched as the last of the deer disappeared into the smoke. "Looks like we're not the only ones trying to get out of here." He shook his head in disgust. This was a bad idea; he should have made them all wait this out at his garage or the motel. He was beginning to wonder if they were going to make it out of here. There were times when the wind blew just right so that the road was completely covered with smoke and flames. He wanted to go faster, but it was impossible to do so safely and would have been foolish.

Thanks to the abandoned cars on the road and the drifting smoke, it took all his concentration to stay out of trouble and avoid hitting something. He really wished he had a way of communicating with the kids. Maybe they had given up and gone back to the garage. But he knew that was wishful thinking. Cy wasn't the type to give up easily and had a tendency to be downright stubborn when it came to tackling a challenge. And while that wasn't normally a bad thing, it could be dangerous now. He just hoped that determination didn't get them into trouble. If anything happened to either one of them, he wouldn't be able to forgive himself.

They continued to inch their way toward the north end of town, where Vince's shop and the motel were located. Except for the occasional gasp, Mary was still silent, and Vince didn't blame her. It was a lot to take in, and it was hard to believe that their hometown and everything they knew had been reduced to this hellish wasteland so quickly.

The drive to the shop this morning had been so peaceful. The summer seemed full of hope and opportunity. Vince had been looking forward to this time with Cy for so long. Now, in a matter of hours, all those hopes and plans had been laid to ruin.

He felt Mary's hand on his arm again, but this time he saw it too. A toppled house completely blocked the street in front of them. Vince stopped the car and took it in for a minute, thinking about the best way around. He considered driving through the yard on the other side of the street, but the heat was too intense, and as he angled the car toward the far side of the road and started to plot a course around the collapsed house, the wind picked up. The sudden gust coaxed the burning debris into a frenzy of swirling embers that headed directly toward them. Before he could react, the paint on the hood began to blister and brown. As soon as he realized what was happening, he slammed the wagon into reverse and spun the wheels on the ash-covered road. He didn't slow down until he put a good distance between them and the fire.

Vince let out a deep breath, followed by a cough. "That was close," he said. "We're going to find another way."

Mary shook her head and squeezed his arm again, only softer this time. The look in her eyes said it all. She was as scared as he was, something neither would admit to the other. What had he gotten them into?

· 15 ·

Vince cranked the wheel hard and got them turned around as quickly as he could. Mary hung on to Nugget to keep her from sliding off the seat as Vince whipped the old wagon around. Afraid that the other burning houses would soon fall as well, he was determined to drive as fast as he could and get them out of there. At least they hadn't blown a tire, something he worried about since the start. With all the loose debris and hot embers on the road, it was a legitimate concern. If they were trapped in this neighborhood and its narrow streets, they would be done for. With no one to put these fires out or at least control them, all the houses would come down eventually; it was just a matter of time. With small yards and streets that barely had enough room for two cars to pass at the same time, they could easily get trapped. If the fire didn't get them, the smoke surely would.

"Be careful!" Mary gripped the door handle with one hand and Nugget with the other.

"I'm trying, but we've got to get out of here." Vince steered the car around two abandoned vehicles on the road and took the next turn onto Lewis Avenue. If they could get to the end of this street, they would hit North Main and be in the clear.

Despite the smoke and poor visibility, Vince pushed well beyond his comfort level of speed for the conditions. He knew it wasn't safe, but there was no alternative. This was an older section of town, and some of the houses were a hundred years old or more. The old structures were going up like matchsticks in a bonfire.

"Vince!" Mary pointed to an old two-story home ahead on the right side of the street.

"I see it." Vince glanced at the house but quickly turned his attention back to the road. The house leaned toward the road at a precarious angle and threatened to topple any second. Vince hugged the left side of the road as far as he dared without getting too close to the houses on the other side. Against his better judgment, he sped up even more. At this point, he was driving from memory as he followed the curve in the road. The bright orange needle on the speedometer climbed well past a safe speed for the roads in this neighborhood, even under good circumstances.

He gripped the wheel firmly and leaned over it as he scanned the road ahead. He couldn't see more than twenty yards or so through the smoke. Operating on pure instinct now, he half-braced himself for impact with an abandoned car or pile of burning rubble. The heat from the fires was a constant reminder of the penalty they would pay if he made the wrong move. This wasn't what he had in mind when he set out to save Mary. The rescue had turned into a nightmare drive-thru hell.

Vince prayed the tires would hold up under the strain and the heat. For the speed he was driving, it took far too long to reach the end of the street. He heard an explosion behind him and flinched.

"What was that? More bombs?" Mary asked.

"It could have been a car or a natural gas tank. Most of these houses have gas tanks outside." He hadn't thought of that until now. The houses around here used natural gas as a primary heating fuel. Some had underground tanks, but a lot of them had smaller above-ground tanks. They might as well be time bombs placed randomly around the neighborhood. Some years back, he saw something on the news about a house in Indianapolis that had been blown to splinters by a faulty gas tank. The explosion had done damage to homes as far away as a block and a half down the street. Even if only three or four of the homes on a street had gas tanks, it would be enough to level the whole block.

Finally, he saw the end of the street approaching. He slowed the car and prepared for a sharp left turn onto North Main. At least the road was wider here and gave him more room to maneuver around any obstacles.

As Vince made the turn and Nugget slid across the slick vinyl seat into Mary, once again another explosion sounded, this time closer. Vince felt the bass of the shockwave in his chest and noticed a fireball rising into the sky off to their left.

"Whoa!" Mary flinched as she hung on to Nugget. For a brief moment, the burst of flames illuminated the sky through the dense smoke-filled air, then subsided and disappeared behind a row of burning buildings. Another good reason to get somewhere safe and wait this out—not that they needed another reason. Somehow, it was getting worse by the minute.

Any survivors would have to make do wherever they were. There was nothing Vince and Mary could do for anyone now, at least not without running the risk of becoming victims of the fires as well. He hated to even think about it, but the phrase crept into his mind before he could stop it. It truly was every man for himself now, whether they liked it or not.

His priority was getting back to the north end of town and finding Cy and the rest of them. If the others weren't back yet, he would drop Mary off and head back out to look for them. That was the only thing worth risking his life for now, but he wouldn't put her at risk again.

They would have to make do with the supplies they had and what they could scavenge when the fires died down. He had a lot of useful things at his house, but he didn't want to get his hopes up. The chances of his house surviving were slim to none. He put the thought out of his mind and concentrated on the road ahead. There was plenty of time to think about that later. Right now, he needed to get them back safe and sound or none of it would matter.

· 16 ·

Vince continued to make his way north on Main Street, dodging burning wrecks and newly fallen buildings that had collapsed and scattered debris onto the road. They were lucky enough to avoid any more close calls—at least nothing like what they experienced in the residential neighborhood they managed to escape minutes earlier.

After what seemed like an eternity, through drifting smoke Vince caught sight of the motel ahead.

"I see the motel!"

Not only did he see the motel, but he also saw the old Toyota pickup that Cy and Reese were driving. He also spotted Jim's Jeep in the parking lot. Jim worked nights at the motel and manned the front desk in case there were any late-night travelers who needed to check in. The van that Fred and Hannah had been using, however, was absent from the parking lot, and that gave him cause for concern. He hoped they were okay and wondered if maybe they had tried to go back to their house in Quincy, although he doubted they would try to drive that far in a van with a bad transmission or without their daughter, Reese. Hopefully they hadn't broken down somewhere out there in this chaos. Getting stranded in one of the tighter residential sections in the middle of town would be a death sentence.

As he pulled into the motel parking lot, Vince couldn't help but feel more than a little guilty about sending them out in the poorly running van. He glanced over at his garage, just to verify that it was still there. Fortunately, it sat alone on a large lot, far enough away from the many burning buildings that it wasn't at risk from the fire jumping between structures. That was probably the only reason the motel had survived as well. Being surrounded by the asphalt parking lot saved it from the spreading fires.

Vince parked next to the pickup truck and turned the wagon off. He let out a deep sigh and looked over at Mary.

"You did good," Mary said, flashing a slight smile. "We made it." Nugget sat up high and looked around, clearly relieved to be out of the thick smoke. The air was still heavy with ash and drifting particles, but it was nowhere near as bad as when they were in the thick of it.

"Dad!" Cy called out. He and Reese made their way out of the closest motel room and headed toward them.

"Have you seen my parents?" Reese asked.

"No, I haven't." Vince made eye contact with Reese as he got out of the car, the feeling of guilt washing over him once more. She wore a look of concern, and rightfully so.

Cy shook his head. "We found a few people and managed to save some supplies from the drug store before it went up. We tried to go back out but we didn't get far. The smoke was too thick and a lot of places are starting to come down. It's bad out there."

"You did the right thing," Vince said.

Mary put her hand on Reese's shoulder. "I'm sure your parents are all right, honey. They probably decided to hunker down somewhere safe and wait it out. The smoke is just too thick to drive through right now."

Reese had a faraway look in her eyes as she glanced back toward town. "I hope you're right."

Just then Buster came tearing out of the motel room, barking and snorting at the new dog. Buster circled Nugget a few times before stopping to get a good sniff of the newcomer. Nugget responded with a few playful barks, then gave Buster a good going-over with her nose. Both dogs' tails wagged as they went around in circles, and Vince was glad to see they were getting along.

They all started for the motel room, where the others were hiding out from the smoke-filled air. When they entered the room, Jim was sitting in a chair next to the window and looking out toward town. Tom and Beverly were sitting with their son, Ryan, on the bed. He was off the oxygen now and sleeping peacefully. Tom carefully got off the bed so as to not wake their son and came over to greet Vince and Mary.

"Major, it's so good to see you guys," Tom said in a hushed voice.

"Glad to see you made it," Vince replied.

"All thanks to your son and Reese." Tom looked at the kids and smiled before glancing back at his sleeping son. Beverly got up carefully and joined them near the door.

"Did you find anyone else?" she asked.

Mary shook her head. "No, we were lucky to make it back ourselves. You can't see twenty feet in front your face out there."

Jim stood up from his chair at the window and joined them. "Is there anything left of the town? What are we going to do?" he asked.

"Let's go next door and talk." Vince looked over at the young boy on the bed as he turned restlessly onto his side. They made their way out of the cramped room and went next door. Buster and

Nugget led the way and investigated the piles of supplies from the pharmacy, which were scattered around the room.

"Wow, you guys did pretty good." Vince patted Cy on the back as he looked at Reese.

"Thanks. We got lucky. I still need to organize it and take inventory of what we have exactly. We were in a hurry, and toward the end, I was grabbing anything I could get my hands on." Reese looked at the hastily formed piles of medical supplies.

"Well you did good. Better than us," Mary added.

"I'm afraid there isn't much left in town, and by the time the fire runs its course, I don't know that there will be anything left standing. Mary's house survived, so there must be others, but for right now, we need to assume that this is all we have," Vince cautioned.

"I have a lot of canned goods in my basement, enough to last us all a couple months if we're careful," Mary offered.

"Thanks, Mary. We're going to need everything we can get our hands on. I have a lot of canned goods in my basement, not to mention a case of MREs I use for hunting trips. Of course, I have no idea if I still have a house." Vince's gut wrenched at the thought.

"Well, I know we lost everything." Beverly's eyes teared up as she spoke. Tom put his arm around her and pulled her close.

"You can all stay here as long as you want," Jim said.

"Thanks, Jim," Vince said. "We're going to need to stay put for a while. It's just not safe out there right now. There's bound to be more survivors and they're going to need our help when things settle down." Vince was about to suggest they all find a spot in the adjacent motel rooms and get some rest while they waited out the fire, but the sound of grinding metal outside interrupted him.

"What's that?" Cy asked as they filed out the door to see what was making the noise. It was coming from the direction of town, and it was getting closer by the second. Slowly but surely, the shape of a van emerged from the smoke. The van wasn't going very fast and the front left wheel was missing the tire, causing the rim to make a horrible noise against the road surface and occasionally throwing a spark or two as it ground into the asphalt.

"It's my parents. They made it!" Reese blurted out.

The van limped into the parking lot and came to a sudden halt a few feet from the entrance. Coughing, Fred jumped out of the driver's side and ran around to open the passenger door.

"Help me!" he yelled as he struggled to pull Hannah out of the seat, her limp body awkwardly held in place with the seat belt. Reese was the first to run toward them, and the others followed close behind.

When Vince reached the van, he noticed the extent of the damage to the vehicle. Nearly all the paint on the left side had been blistered off by the heat and was still smoking. Cy and Tom took over pulling Hannah out of the seat since Fred, unable to continue supporting her weight, doubled over in a fit of coughing. They carried her to the motel while Vince helped Fred stay on his feet and follow them to the room. He glanced back at the battered and smoking van. How would he face Reese if her mother didn't make it? How would he face any of them? This was his fault. He never should have sent them out there in the first place.

· 17 ·

"Take her to 102!" Reese shouted as she ran ahead to the room and opened the door. She dug through the pile of supplies until she found an oxygen tank and a mask. By the time Cy and Tom came through the door with Hannah and laid her on the nearest bed, she was ready with the mask.

"Don't lay her flat. Keep her on her side," Reese barked as she placed two pillows behind her mother to prevent her from rolling over onto her back. She secured the mask around her head and positioned it over her nose and mouth. Reese noticed the soot and knew right away that her mother was dealing with smoke inhalation. She hoped it wasn't bad enough to cause swelling and close off the airways; otherwise, her mother would have to be intubated. That was something she had never done. Intubation was the process of forcing a tube down the victim's throat in order to bypass any swelling caused by the inhalation of carcinogens and particles in the smoke. If the respiratory distress was bad enough, there was also a danger of the victim breathing in the contents of their own stomach or mucus caused by the irritation of the airways.

The condensation that began to accumulate in the clear plastic mask was a welcome sight and gave Reese a small measure of relief. There wasn't much else they could do for her other than let her rest and keep her on oxygen.

"I think she's going to be okay." Reese looked at her dad, who hovered over top of her and kept a watchful eye on his wife as she lay there motionless. Reese felt his hand on her shoulder until he launched into another fit of uncontrollable coughing.

"We need to get you on a tank too. There should still be plenty left in the room next door," she suggested.

"I'll get it. I want to check on Ryan anyway." Hannah headed over to the room next door. Reese looked around the room and decided to speak up for the safety of everyone.

"I don't think any of us need to be exposed to any more smoke today. There's no telling what kinds of things are burning out there and what we're breathing in."

Vince nodded. "She's right. We all need to stay put until things die down. We need to conserve the oxygen tanks we have. There's going to be survivors that will need medical attention and all the resources we have. Driving around out there now is pointless. We're just putting ourselves at risk for nothing if we go back out there. Why don't we let the Morgans have this room? Tom, you and your wife can stay in 101 with your boy. Cy, Mary, and I can crash next door for the time being. That okay with you, Jim?" Vince asked.

"Sure, yeah. I'll go grab the keys."

"Good, it's settled then. We're all in agreement to wait it out here?" Vince asked. Everyone in the room signaled their agreement.

Reese was glad everyone agreed to stay put for the time being. She already felt the pressure of being the only one with any medical training, and these weren't cats and dogs; these were people who were counting on her. The last thing she wanted was more patients. She was already in way over her head, and by the looks of the others, it wouldn't take much more exposure to smoke and airborne particles to push them over the edge of needing medical attention.

She looked at the mess of supplies around the room. She would have her hands full for a while sorting through what they managed to save. She needed to take inventory and keep track of what they had, and she knew she needed to do it now.

Once the fires died out, there would be plenty of

people in need of help, and like it or not, that responsibility would largely fall on her shoulders. She fought off the urge to panic. She wasn't trained for this. With any luck, there would be other survivors who had first aid skills. She couldn't do this on her own, but the reality was that she might have to. She wasn't prepared to have people's lives in her hands. All her training was geared toward animals, and while there were some similarities, a human being was a whole other thing entirely.

Her dad cleared a spot on the bed and put his hand on her shoulder. Was her uneasiness that obvious?

He managed a smile between muffled coughs. "You're doing a good job, honey. We're all lucky to have you here."

Beverly returned with the oxygen tank her son had been using and placed it on the bed next to Fred. "Here you go. Ryan is doing much better." She turned to leave but stopped and looked at Reese. "Thank you again. If it wasn't for you and Cy, our son..." She choked on her words and began to tear up again.

Reese interrupted her before she could continue. "It's okay. We're all in this together," she said.

Beverly nodded and made a hasty exit back to her room. Fred pulled the mask over his face and took a few deep breaths as Reese opened the valve on the tank.

Vince headed for the door. Cy followed but stopped before he walked out of the room. "Well," Vince said, "we'll let you guys get some rest."

"If you need any help with anything, let me know," Cy offered.

"Thanks," Reese answered.

"Come on, girl." Mary urged Nugget to follow them as they headed for the next room. Nugget jumped up from the corner of the room where she had been lying next to Buster and followed obediently. As soon as the door closed, Fred lay down on the bed and closed his eyes as he continued to inhale the much-needed oxygen from the tank. And for the first time since this all began, it was quiet.

Reese looked over her mother and ran her fingers through her soot-covered hair. Brushing pieces of ash from her mother's curls, she tried to make sense of all that had happened. But it was too much to comprehend. She knew in her heart that she would never return to school and that life as she knew it had changed forever. She felt a deep sadness begin to creep over her as she thought about all the friends she would most likely never see again and their fates in all this. The sadness turned to anger when she thought about all the lives that had been lost. The truth was, everyone she'd ever known was gone from her life.

A familiar cold nose nudging her elbow and forcing its way under her arm interrupted her thoughts. Buster was still here, and so were her parents. Things could be worse—a lot worse. She tried to focus on what she still had as she scratched Buster behind his ears, his eyes closing in satisfaction and his head coming to rest on her leg.

This was a new world and she was going to have to make the best of it. She still didn't know if she was up for the challenge, but she was determined to try her best and help out in any way she could. They would all have to work together. It was the only way any of them would survive.

· 18 ·

Vince was glad to see Jim coming down the walkway with room keys in his hand. He was anxious to get inside and close the door. There was nothing they could do about the smell, but at least inside the room, with the door shut, they could eliminate the smoke and breathe a little easier, although they might never get the burnt smell out of their hair and clothing.

It wasn't the type of smoke that came off a campfire or wood-burning fireplace. It was a harsh, toxic, soot-laden smoke that seemed to pierce all the senses. It left a foul taste in his mouth, and he was thankful for the water that Mary brought from her house. The water helped soothe his throat and wash away the burning sensation.

Water was going to be one of the top priorities when things settled down. Unfortunately, the motel, like most things in town, was on city water. Even if he could get the power back up and running using the solar panels at his garage, it wouldn't solve their water problem at the motel. He knew there were a few freshwater springs around town, so maybe they could set up a pump and some hoses to bring water to the motel. But that was something to worry about later. For the time being, they would have to carry water in containers from the garage if he could get the well pump working.

Jim opened up the door to room 103 and put two sets of room keys on the table next to the small TV. "I'll stay in the office. There's a cot in the back room. That's where I usually sleep during the night shift anyway." Jim started for the door.

"Thanks for letting us all use the motel," Mary said.

"Heck, it's the least I can do. We're all in this together. Right, Major?" Jim glanced at Cy nervously before he looked at Vince, as if he was waiting for approval.

"That's right," Vince answered. The truth was, whether Jim cooperated or not, they were going to stay there. What choice did they have?

"Okay, well I guess I'll see you guys later." Jim closed the door behind him and passed by the window on his way back to the front office.

Nugget leapt up onto one of the double beds and made a few circles over a spot before she lay down with a sigh.

"Well, I guess we'll take this one," Mary said as she let out a small cough.

"Sounds good." Vince looked at his watch. "Can't believe it's almost noon."

Cy glanced out the window. "It sure doesn't feel like it. Looks a lot later than that."

He was right. The sun was nothing more than a pale-yellow spot in the sky, barely visible through the smoke and ash-filled air. If Vince didn't know what time it was, it could have passed for the moon on a cloudy night. The light that managed to filter through and make its way into the room cast an unnatural shade of yellow over everything.

Vince wondered how long it would be before they saw clear blue skies again. He knew it wasn't just their town that looked like this. If the rest of the country was going through the same scenario and dealing with fires, it would be a long time before the atmosphere returned to normal.

"I guess we might as well get some rest." Cy sat down at the edge of the bed and took his shoes off.

Vince sighed. "Yeah, I suppose so." It wasn't like there was anything else they could do right now. He initially thought about going back to the garage to see if he could get the power working, but given the lack of sunlight, he had his doubts about the solar panels providing much electricity. There would only be enough power in the storage batteries to run a few things. Right now, getting some rest was the best option. God knew there was plenty of work ahead of them. Not to mention, doing anything outside meant breathing in the toxic air, and they had all done enough of that as it was.

Vince sat down on the bed opposite of Cy and lay back on the pillows. He glanced over at Mary, who already had her eyes shut. Nugget had moved from her spot at the foot of the bed and was snuggled up next to Mary's side. Cy was staring up at the ceiling quietly and no doubt deep in thought as he tried to process all that had happened in the last few hours.

They were all covered in a layer of soot, and as Vince rubbed his face and looked at the black and gray filth on his hands, he was reminded again about the lack of amenities. How nice it would have been to clean up a little. They would have to use containers for now and go find water when they ventured out again. Staying hydrated was important, but they also needed to clean themselves up.

Vince wasn't looking forward to sorting through the aftermath of the fires, and as he lay there, his thoughts drifted to all the people that hadn't made it. Hopefully they would find more survivors. They were going to need all the help they could get for sorting through what was left of their town. He thought about Bill and wondered what had become of him. When the bombs hit, he must have gone home to find his wife and daughter. With any luck, he'd arrived in time to save them from the fate of so many others. For the time being, Vince had to believe that Bill was successful and that he and his family were waiting it out somewhere safe.

And what about his good friend John? Surely he was all right and had survived. He probably ran home as well to save his family. Oh, how Vince hoped there were other people who survived the attacks. He didn't want the burden or responsibility of being in charge of what was left. But he could feel the stares from the others already. They looked to him for answers and guidance on what to do next. He didn't have any answers and he didn't want to be that person.

Vince rubbed at his eyes. He could feel the pressure and the sense of responsibility building. There was so much to do that the thought alone made him tired. He tried to focus on the positive. He had his son and Mary safe and sound by his side, at least for the time being. These were the people who mattered most in his life, and he was beyond fortunate to have them both. They faced an uphill battle, the struggle would be real, and it was going to be hard, but together, they would make it. They had to.

· 19 ·

Bang, bang, bang. The noise at the door startled Vince. Nugget followed it up with a few barks and growls as she shot up and stood at the edge of Mary's bed.

The door cracked open to reveal a distressed and excited Jim. "Major," he said, "there's someone driving through town."

"I'm coming. Hang on." Vince rubbed at his eyes, forgetting that his face was coated in soot. He quickly remembered by the gritty feel on his cheeks and hands. His eyes burned and felt irritated, no doubt from the grime and ash that covered him from head to toe. He sat up and put on his boots but didn't bother to tie the laces. Staggering over to the door, he glanced back at Cy and Mary, who were still asleep despite the racquet Tom and Nugget had made.

"What's going on?" Vince squinted in the dim light as his eyes adjusted. He pulled the door open far enough to step into the still thick and heavy air, then pulled it closed softly behind him. Checking his watch, he saw that it was five o'clock already. That surprised him, and if he had to guess how long he'd been out, he would have bet no more than a few minutes.

The world outside slowly came into focus—or at least what he could see of it. The smoke hadn't dissipated much, and the smell of the burning fires was still strong. He hadn't expected it to improve for a couple of days, but seeing it all firsthand again was a painful reminder of the morning's events. For a brief moment when he first woke up, he wondered if it had all been a bad dream. But the view outside the motel shattered that illusion and the reality of his situation came flooding back in waves.

Jim looked anxious, like he was going to burst if he didn't get out what he had to say. He nervously glanced between Vince and the road in front of the motel. Whatever was going on had him pretty worked up.

"Well, what's going on?" Vince stretched as he tried to work out a pain in his back.

"Two cars and an old pickup truck drove through a couple minutes ago. Then another pickup with two more people came a little later. They stopped in front of your garage for a bit, but then they moved on when the last truck pulled in.

The guy in the last truck said something to the guy driving the lead car and they all left together in a hurry." Jim wrung his hands as he shifted his weight restlessly from one foot to the other.

While Vince began to process the information, he couldn't help but wonder why Jim seemed so nervous. After all that had happened today, a few cars driving around was hardly news worth getting worked up over, and there were bound to be other survivors out there.

Vince thought of Bill. "Was one of them a Dodge pickup?"

"No, but the thing is, they had guns." Jim stopped moving around and made direct eye contact with Vince for the first time since he started talking. Now Vince knew why he was so worked up.

"What do you mean? Guns? Who were they?" Vince was wide awake now and firing on all cylinders.

"There were six guys and then another two in the truck that came in later, but they didn't see me. I got down on the floor and watched them from behind the counter. Not all of them were carrying guns, but at least three were from what I could see," Jim spat in one breath.

"Did they take any interest in the motel?" Vince asked.

"I don't think so. Two of them walked over and

looked around the gas pumps at your place. They were both carrying shotguns. The other guy had what looked like an AR-15, but he stayed out on the road near the vehicles." Jim began pacing again.

"Which way did they go when they left?" Vince asked.

Jim pointed. "Back toward the interstate, the way they came in."

Vince sighed. "How long ago did you see all this?"

"I woke you up as soon as they left," Jim answered. "Do you think they'll come back?"

"Probably," Vince said.

There was no *probably* to it, though, and Vince knew it. They'd be back sooner rather than later. If it wasn't for the contents of his store, it would be for the gas. He never imagined that they would run into trouble this quickly. He thought people would be preoccupied with self-preservation for at least a couple of days. But here it was, less than a day in, and things had deteriorated to lawlessness and roving gangs of armed looters, which was no doubt what Jim had seen. You don't drive around with weapons at the ready if you're looking to rescue people. They would have to assume the worst and be ready for them if they came back.

Vince thought for a minute about their situation. Jim had a revolver and Vince had his .45 and an old shortened 12-gauge shotgun he kept behind the counter at the garage. Jim said three of them were carrying guns, but Vince would put money on the rest of the gang being armed as well. It would be foolish to assume otherwise. If it came to a straight-out gunfight, they would be outgunned for sure. Maybe they should try and avoid them altogether for now if they could, but Vince knew that wasn't a solution and that an encounter with the armed group was inevitable.

"Do you have any more weapons around here?" Vince asked.

"No, this is it." Jim put his hand on the large revolver tucked into his waistband. Vince figured as much, but there was no harm in asking. Making a run to his house or Mary's was out of the question and probably not worth it right now. Considering how things were going, he might not even be able to go to either place. The roads were most likely impassable and covered with debris from the collapsed buildings. Surely a lot more had come down since this morning.

If Vince did manage to make it to his place, there was no guarantee that it hadn't burned to the ground like most everything else. Even if the safe had done its job and protected the contents, it would be too hot to touch, assuming it wasn't buried under the remains of the house.

He would have to address that in the near future: clearing the roads and sorting through the collapsed buildings to look for anything they could use to help them survive. He thought of the Massey Ferguson in the barn but quickly dismissed the idea. It was probably buried and burned. Besides, the tractor wasn't big enough for the job. Vince would need something bigger.

The Cloverdale quarry had a few pieces of equipment, including a large articulated loader. Vince had seen it shuttling buckets of gravel across the yard on more than one occasion. The bigger question was, did it still run? It looked like an older piece of equipment, but there was no telling. For now, all of that would have to wait, though. Besides, the quarry was outside of town to the north and several miles past the interstate. Running out there to try and commandeer a piece of equipment would be something Vince and a few volunteers would have to try when they were better organized and could defend themselves. Before attempting anything like that, Vince wanted to be more prepared to deal with the armed and dangerous crew Jim had seen.

"Let's get everybody together in the motel conference room ASAP," Vince said.

Jim nodded and started for the motel to let the others know, but he stopped when he noticed Vince wasn't following him. "Where are you going, Major?"

"I'm going to get that shotgun while I can. We're going to need it. I'll be back in a couple minutes and meet you all in the conference room."

"Want me to come with you?" Jim asked.

"No, I need you to get everybody moving and let them know what's going on. Wait for me there and stay out of sight, no matter what. Got it?"

"Got it." Jim turned and was on his way without asking any more questions, and Vince was glad. The clock was ticking, and his opportunity to get across the street and back without running into the armed group was slipping away. He guessed the only reason they hadn't stayed and looted his shop was because they found something better. They'd be back once they cleaned out wherever they were. But with any luck and a little time, Vince and the others would be ready for them. They couldn't afford to roll over and let these looters take what they wanted. It was time to make a stand and fight for what was theirs.

· 20 ·

Before heading to the garage, Vince stopped at his car and took his holstered pistol out from under the seat. It was foolish of him to have left it there and he was disappointed in himself for doing so. Things would have gone very badly if the looters had taken an interest in the motel or their vehicles. He was going to have to do better than that. No more letting his guard down.

He slid the concealed carry holster and the pistol onto his belt at the small of his back. He preferred to carry it there, as it made for quick retrieval with his right hand. The .45 would remain with him from now on, and he'd like to see the others armed as well—eventually.

That was one of the things he planned on discussing with the group when he got back. He wasn't sure how many of them knew how to handle a gun or, for that matter, what their experience level was, but they needed to be armed and able to defend themselves.

He knew Cy was a good shot and competent with a weapon. When he visited, they enjoyed taking the guns out back and doing some target-shooting. Of course, targets didn't shoot back, and confronting a person with a gun or protecting yourself was entirely different than shooting steel plates at one hundred yards.

Jim had the pistol, although having a gun and knowing how to use it didn't necessarily go together. And then there was Mary, who Vince knew was good with a shotgun. But he had no idea about the others. If they didn't know how to use a gun, they'd have to learn fast. If he could get to his safe and get Mary's shotgun, they'd have enough weapons to arm everyone. As crazy as that sounded, it was the way things were now.

Vince closed up the wagon and headed for the garage. He was a pretty active guy and in good shape for his age, but the run from the motel to his garage across the street winded him. It had been a long time since he'd run anywhere, and it showed. Reaching into his pocket, he pulled out his keys and breathed deeply to regain his composure. He pulled the door open and slipped inside as fast as he could. The thought of the looters returning any minute now nagged at him, and he didn't want to get caught there.

As much as he wanted to get the power back on, there was no time for that now. Not to mention, any artificial light coming from the garage would only serve to draw attention. Attention was something he needed to avoid right now—and maybe always from here on out. The interstate was barely visible from the shop, but once the fires died down, even a small amount of light would give it away in the darkness. There was no need to advertise the fact that Vince and the other survivors had amenities.

Vince made his way behind the counter and reached under the register until he felt the butt of the shotgun. It was an old 12-gauge Remington pump he'd picked up at a yard sale. It wasn't pretty, but that was one of the reasons he originally bought it, and he didn't feel bad about trimming a few inches off the barrel, just past the magazine. The shortened barrel allowed him to keep it under the register. It also served another purpose: it caused the buckshot to spread out quicker and make a larger pattern in less distance. It was ideal for self-defense at short range and in a small area. After he modified the barrel, he had tried it out behind his house and was pleased to see a four- to five-foot spread on the buckshot at about thirty yards. Of course, this limited the gun's usefulness at greater distances, but that was okay, considering its intended use.

The modified shotgun wasn't exactly legal, but he didn't see the harm since it was a permanent fixture here and never left the shop. He kept the gun loaded with double-aught buckshot. Each shotgun shell contained fifteen small steel balls that would tear through just about anything at fifty yards or less. He'd never had to use the gun, but Vince was a firm believer in the motto of "better to have it and not need it than to need it and not have it." With the recent break-ins around town, it seemed more and more like a better idea every day.

With a pump of the foregrip, he chambered a shell in the gun and flipped the safety on. The sound echoed through the empty store and reminded Vince how serious the situation was. He grabbed a flashlight off the shelf behind the counter and headed back to his office. Careful to keep the flashlight pointed down and only use it when necessary, he made his way through the darkness.

Once he was in his office, he sat down in the chair behind his desk and opened the drawer containing the shotgun shells. He eyed the bottle of whiskey next to the box of ammo. For a moment, he thought about taking a shot to help calm his nerves but decided against it. He needed his wits about him right now, and although it might settle him down a bit, it wouldn't help the situation. He grabbed the box of shells and closed the drawer before he changed his mind.

He needed to get back to the motel and come up with a plan for dealing with the looters. He'd already been here too long as it was and he didn't want one of the others to come looking for him. He was about to get up from behind the desk when heard a vehicle outside.

Too late. They were back.

Vince froze. Halfway out of his chair, he leaned on the desk and listened to the exhaust note grow louder. It sounded like a single car or truck and he was thankful for that, but it didn't help slow his now rapidly beating heart. Setting the box of shells down quietly on the desk, he stood up and moved out from behind it. He approached the door to his office, gripping the shotgun with both hands and holding it at the ready.

With any luck, whoever it was would pass by the garage, but that was wishful thinking. His fears were soon confirmed, and a bright beam from the headlights cut through the darkness of the storefront. Vince followed the light with his eyes as it spilled down the hallway and in through his office door.

Crouching down, he made his way to the end of the hallway, then crawled the last couple feet to get behind the counter. He eased up from his lowered position just far enough to peer over the counter and see out the front windows, but he ducked back down when, to his disappointment, the vehicle pulled directly into the garage lot and parked out front. Vince was momentarily blinded by a series of extremely bright white LED off-road lights mounted to a truck. He heard the brakes squeal as the truck came to a stop in front of the store. The brightness of the lights made it impossible to see what kind of truck it was or who was in it.

If there were only a few of them, his best chance would be to get them as they grouped up and came through the front door, which he now regretted leaving unlocked. At this distance, the buckshot would have enough spread to cover the doorway, and it had enough power behind it to take them all out at once. If he timed it right and held his cool, he could do it with one shot. He'd wait until they were inside the store. He wasn't happy about not knowing who it was, though, and hated the idea of shooting blindly. What if it was someone he knew from town or survivors looking for help?

He prepared to spring into action and bring the gun up to the counter as he heard the truck door open and then close. *Only one door. That's good.* Maybe it wasn't the intruders after all. Even if it was, he could handle one of them a lot more easily than a group. He eased the gun onto the counter until it lay across the smooth Formica top and pointed toward the entrance. He got behind the shotgun and seated the butt of it against his shoulder as he crouched down and aimed at the doorway. He could make out the silhouette of a man wearing a ball cap. He could also see that he was carrying a scoped rifle. Vince would have the advantage. The long rifle would be difficult to use in these close quarters and the scope would only be a hindrance at this range. The man would have to shoot from the hip.

Vince licked at his chapped lips but got no relief; his mouth was dry and tasted like ash. He watched as the dark figure opened the door and stepped inside. Vince slowly slid his finger down to the trigger. His adrenaline pumped as he prepared to do whatever was necessary. It had been a long time since he stared at another human being down the barrel of a gun. He hadn't forgotten that feeling and by no means missed it.

· 21 ·

"Major?" The familiar voice cut the tension like a knife, and Vince felt a sense of relief wash over him. It was Bill; he'd come back to the garage.

"Major, you in here?" Bill called out again before Vince had a chance to answer.

"Yeah, I'm here behind the counter." Vince took his finger off the trigger and slid the gun off the countertop. He took a few deep breaths as Bill moved toward him and blocked the glaring lights with his body, enough for Vince to see him now. Of course it was Bill; he should have known. The image of Bill's one-ton four-wheel drive Dodge pickup with the LED-mounted lightbar flashed in his head.

"You gave me a good scare there, buddy," Vince said. He didn't want to let on how close he had been to pulling the trigger, and the thought sent chills down his spine.

"It's good to see you, Major. I thought you were a goner. Can you believe all this?" Bill looked outside.

"It's good to see you too. We barely made it back from Indy," Vince said.

"I know. I just talked to your boy over at the motel. I saw your wagon and went there first. They told me you were over here and filled me in on what's going on. I thought you could use a hand in case those people came back." Bill motioned with his rifle.

"What about your family?" Vince asked reluctantly.

Bill nodded. "I got to the girls in time. I left them with the others at the motel." Bill paused and looked down for a second. "The house is a loss, though. We managed to grab a few things and my rifle, but that's about it, I'm afraid. We were luckier than most, from the looks of things."

Vince was relieved to hear that Bill's wife, Sarah, and their little girl, Sasha, had been spared. "You are lucky," Vince said.

A distant explosion sounded and brought Vince back to reality.

"We need to get out of here, Bill. I just came over for the shotgun. Turn your lights off and keep an eye out, will you, while I grab something." Vince didn't wait for a response and ran back to his office for the box of shotgun shells. They were pushing their luck with Bill's truck out front. With those LEDs reflecting off the front of the building, they might as well have a flashing neon sign out front that said, *Here we are. Come and get us.*

When Vince returned. Bill was no longer inside the store and was back in his truck, the lights off and the motor running. Vince paused for a second and looked around. Were they being foolish by leaving all these supplies here? Now that Bill was here with his truck, should they quickly load as much as they could into the pickup and take it with them? Vince hated the thought of someone looting his store and making off with all these supplies. He also hated the idea of bugging out of his own place, and the thought made him feel like they were running scared. But before he could make a decision, Bill leaned out of the truck window.

"Major, somebody's coming from the interstate. We gotta' go!" Bill frantically waved his hand, motioning for Vince to hurry up.

Vince forgot about the supplies and started for the truck. Before he ran out the door, it dawned on him that he and Bill couldn't afford to try and make a getaway back to the motel. If they did that and were spotted, then they would be giving away the location of the others. Even with the addition of Bill and his rifle, they were outgunned and outnumbered. From what Jim had said, Vince figured the whole gang of intruders was armed and dangerous. Vince and the others only had four weapons in total, and two of them were pistols and one a short-range shotgun.

No, he and Bill would have to make a stand right here, right now.

"Bill, shut the truck down and get out. We can't risk leading them over to the motel."

"We're staying here? I mean, what are we gonna do?" Bill had a confused and worried look on his face.

"We're staying put. We'll fight them here, if it comes to that." Vince hoped there was another way out of this—one that didn't involve a fight—but he knew otherwise. What else would they be coming back for? The rest of the town was burned down. There was nothing else here for them other than the supplies in his store.

"Look, we don't have a choice, Bill. This garage full of tools, the solar electric system, and all the supplies here. We need this place to survive. Without it, we're lost. I don't know what you've seen in your travels today, but there's nothing left out there. There's nowhere to run."

Bill turned the truck off and hopped out, his rifle in hand. He walked around to the front, where Vince stood and looked him in the eye. "I'm with you, Major," Bill said. "What's the plan?"

"All right, first we need to get into defendable positions. They're going to see a truck that wasn't here last time and figure someone is inside the building. I want you to go across the street on foot, but stop in the parking lot and get under the van parked out by the curb. Make sure you can see the garage from where you set up. I just want you to cover me. If we hit them from a couple different directions, it will confuse them and make them think there are more of us than there are. Understand?"

"Yeah, I think so."

"All right. Get going. The smoke will cover you." Vince looked down the road to see if he could make out the approaching cars, but the drifting smoke still mostly obscured the lights. He estimated they were still a mile or so away and moving slowly due to the poor visibility. They'd never see a single person cross the street in this low light and drifting smoke, but the big red and white Dodge would surely draw their attention. Bill stood there with a blank look on his face.

"Go! Now!" Vince barked.

Bill jumped at the sound of his voice and took off running toward the motel parking lot. Vince felt bad about shouting, but this was no time to worry about hurt feelings. This was do or die. Without wasting any time, Vince headed through the gate that led to the rear yard behind his shop. At the back of his building, a permanently affixed ladder ran up to the flat roof. He'd been up there many times before to perform maintenance on the solar panel system and repair a few leaks.

As he climbed the ladder, he ran through a few scenarios in his mind and decided his best chance was to hit them first and hit them hard. He would have the element of surprise and needed to capitalize on that. Best-case scenario, that would scare the looters into a retreat and then they would run. Worst-case, Vince and Bill would have a gunfight on their hands, but at least they could take a few of the looters out early. It probably wasn't the best plan, but it was the one Vince had come up with in the time he had, and he was going with it.

Vince couldn't believe he was going over these things in his head as he reached the top of the ladder and climbed up onto the flat part of the roof. It was a parapet-style roof, and as a result, there was a section of wall that extended three feet above the flat surface on the front and sides of the building. It made the building look taller than it actually was.

Vince always considered it a poor design and, in general, a pain in the butt since it was prone to developing leaks where the exterior wall and flat area met. But now, he was thankful for the extra three feet of concrete block that ran up past the roofline. It would allow him to stay hidden and provide cover when he launched his surprise attack on the unsuspecting looters.

Vince ran to the edge of the roof and got into position behind the wall. He pulled the .45 from its holster and set it by his feet, along with the box of shotgun shells. He had four rounds of double-aught buckshot loaded in the gun's magazine and one in the chamber from before. He pulled an extra shell from the box and slid it into the magazine to top it off. Between the shotgun and his pistol, which held only held seven rounds, he would have to be choosy with his shots. What he would have given to have the .308 Scout with him, but he didn't. He'd have to make do with the shotgun primarily and fall back to the pistol while he reloaded from the box of shells.

Vince glanced at the headlights down the road as they grew closer, then looked over to see if he could spot Bill at his position under the van. He could barely make out the van from where he was, let alone see if Bill had followed his instructions and hid under underneath it. The smoke was thicker on the roof than it was on the ground, and although it was a lot less pleasant to breathe, he was thankful for the added cover.

Since this was supposed to be a quick trip over to retrieve the shotgun, he hadn't brought the mask with him, so he made do by pulling his shirt over his mouth and nose for the time being. He hated to admit it, but the shirt worked just as well as the cheap paper masks everyone had been using. As he sat there and waited, he became aware again of how dry his mouth was. When he swallowed, he tasted ash and soot, reminding him how badly he needed to drink some water.

Among his priorities, water would be at the top of the list when he and the others divided up responsibilities. In fact, it would probably be best if everyone chipped in and made that their mission for the immediate future. Without a clean water source, they would all become dehydrated quickly. The garage water was well fed, though, and that would be their best bet for immediate access to water. Tying the motel into one of the local springs would take some thought and a lot of hard work.

The garage property was developed before the town annexed land that far north, so it wasn't required to tie into city water, and Vince had opted to stick with the well for his water needs. If he could restore power through the solar electric system, then he should be able to power the well pump and draw water. Thinking about this now reminded him why he couldn't afford to lose the garage to a band of roving thugs.

· 22 ·

As Vince watched the lights steadily advance on their location, he began to cough. His throat was dry and it burned every time he swallowed. The humidity must have been close to zero, and Vince wondered if that was due to the bombs exploding in the upper atmosphere or the massive number of fires. Whatever the reason, it was bad and the smoke wasn't helping. He noticed his lips beginning to chap badly, and his hands felt like sandpaper when he rubbed his face. What they needed was a good rainstorm, but he doubted that would happen anytime soon.

Then he had a thought. The rooftop air conditioner units had been running for a couple days now since the weather had turned warm. It was a long shot because they turned off when the bombs detonated early this morning, but there was a chance there was still water in the condensate lines. It was worth a try; even a little bit of water would provide his throat with some much-needed relief. Besides, hiding up on the roof would be all for nothing if he gave himself away by coughing at the wrong time.

Vince hurried over to the first unit and found the PVC drain line. The pipe formed a U shape where it came out of the condenser unit. If there was any water left in the line, that was where it would be. There was a small piece of PVC that stuck off from the bottom of the U and was capped off. This would normally be used as a clean-out point for the condensate line in case of a clog, but today, it would make an ideal faucet. Vince reached into his pocket and pulled out his folding knife as he glanced back toward the road and the oncoming lights. He didn't have much time and needed to work fast. Forcing the blade tip around the edges of the glued-in-place PVC cap, he worked it all the way around the joint. By tapping the knife with the butt of the shotgun, he easily forced the cap loose to the point where he could twist it with his hand. He put the knife away and lay down flat on his back, careful to position his mouth under the clean-out pipe. He closed his eyes as he gave the cap one final twist and pulled it free.

A gush of warm but clean water filled his mouth. He swallowed as quickly as he could but couldn't keep up with the sudden flow of water, so some escaped and ran over his face and down his collar. The water had a plastic taste to it, but he didn't mind. It felt good on his throat and was a welcome change from the dry, irritating sensation that had been tormenting him.

The water stopped flowing as quickly as it had started, and he wiped his face clear of the excess spillage with his T-shirt. When he pulled the shirt away, he wasn't surprised to see the amount of dirt and soot that came off his face. He felt better, but this was no time to sit back and relax. He grabbed the shotgun, returned to the edge of the roof, and resumed his position.

The vehicles were close enough now that he could make out more than just their lights. Some of them weren't cars at all; instead, most of the meandering lights belonged to ATVs. A black Ford pickup led the caravan, followed by a few ATVs. Lastly, a few more ATVs brought up the rear.

Vince was happy to see the four-wheelers in the mix. They were open targets and left their drivers and passengers exposed. If and when the shooting started, they'd be quick to run for cover. That meant he could focus on the pickup and the car.

As they emerged from the smoke one by one, Vince could also see that the ATV operators all had weapons slung over their bodies. Most were shotguns, and a few had assault-style rifles or AR-15s. They also had their faces covered with bandanas or rags and goggles over their eyes, no doubt to protect against smoke and debris in the air.

The fact that they were all armed, even the passengers on the ATVs, confirmed that they meant business. A few of the passengers on the four-wheelers carried bottles of booze. They were taking turns with the bottles and passing them back and forth as they drove dangerously close to one another and crawled toward the garage. At this range, Vince could make out the occasional hoot and holler from some of the riders as they drove erratically down the road.

The Ford pickup slowed and began to make the turn into the garage parking lot, but before it pulled off the road, a man leaned out of the passenger window. He held up a liquor bottle and drained the remainder of the contents in one gulp. Then, with a loud whoop, he tossed the empty bottle into the air and over the back of the truck, toward the ATVs. The first rider in line behind the truck was already stopped and whipped out a pistol from his waistband.

CRACK! CRACK!

The sound of the low-caliber pistol echoed off the front of the building and Vince ducked down behind the block wall instinctively. A moment later, he heard the bottle smash as it landed on the asphalt. When he peered back over the wall and down onto the scene below him, the passenger in the pickup had launched into a profanity-laced tirade directed at the shooter, no doubt in response to the two shots that missed the bottle and sailed past the pickup. The driver of the ATV shouted something back, but the passenger was already back inside the moving truck as it pulled into the lot and made a 180-degree turn.

For a brief moment, Vince thought they changed their minds in the midst of their argument and were leaving. Then he saw the backup lights flash on the pickup. His heart sank a little as he realized they were only positioning the truck to back it up bed-first to the store, making it easier to load what they stole.

Vince wondered if the others had heard the gunshots or the loud revving of the ATVs, but he hoped they hadn't. The last thing he wanted was for anyone to come out of the motel to see what was going on. He had no doubt now that the intruders would be quick to shoot at anyone they deemed a threat. Vince glanced over at Bill's location under the van—or at least where he hoped Bill was—as the rest of the ATVs and the car pulled into the lot. The car parked near the front of the store and close to Bill's truck, but most of the ATVs tore around the parking lot, unnecessarily doing donuts and foolish stunts. If the others back at the motel hadn't heard them yet, they would surely hear this.

After a little while, they settled down and surrounded the pickup and the car. They were all practically underneath Vince now, and from his position on the roof, he had a bird's-eye view of the group. His optimism was bolstered by the relatively short distance between him and the looters and his angle of attack. The tightness of the group also ensured multiple hits with the shotgun at this distance.

There would be no negotiating with these people. They were here to clean out the store and take what they wanted from the garage as well. What they didn't get on this trip they would return for until they had cleaned the place out. And they wouldn't stop there; it would only be a matter of time before they discovered the motel and the others.

Before the caravan of intruders had come into plain view, Vince struggled with the moral dilemma of shooting first and taking a life as opposed to maybe trying to reason with them. But that was no longer a concern, and he knew what he had to do.

· 23 ·

Vince tightened his grip on the shotgun as the tension built. Some of the riders dismounted the ATVs and assembled between the car and the pickup. There didn't appear to be much organization among the group, but there was clearly a pecking order, as they watched the driver of the pickup closely. Vince could see down into the window of the Ford and watched the man at the wheel unwrap a cigar and then stuck it into his mouth. He wore a ball cap and a plaid shirt and took the time to chew on the cigar and talk with his passenger for a moment before he got out and addressed the gathering crowd.

"Listen up, people. We're going to do this a little different from the last place we hit. I want at least three of you to stay outside and keep an eye on things. That's why we ran into trouble last time and lost Junior. Those people never woulda got the jump on us if you'd kept a lookout. And by all

151

means, if you see somebody with a gun, just shoot 'em without hesitating this time, Bobby." The man directed his attention to one of the ATV riders at the outside of the group. Vince assumed that was Bobby and that he'd screwed up at the last place they robbed.

One of the other gang members scolded Bobby. "You're lucky I'm a good shot or they woulda got more than one of us."

A few of the others chimed in and gave their opinions, but Vince wasn't paying attention now. He was slowly and quietly getting ready to take his shot. He'd heard enough to alleviate any feelings of guilt or doubt about what he was preparing to do. These people were killers and thieves and needed to be dealt with accordingly. As Vince began to line up his shot and flick off the safety, out of the corner of his eye he caught some movement from the motel parking lot. But before he could make out who it was, he saw a muzzle flash from the across the street. It was Jim running full tilt across the motel parking lot. What was he thinking?

BOOM!

Then another muzzle flash, this time from under the van, followed instantly by the crack of Bill's rifle. The back window of the car below him exploded in a shower of glass fragments and one of the ATV riders fell to the ground with an agonizing scream.

"I'm hit!" He rolled around on the ground as the others abandoned him. Some ran for cover and some chose instead to head for their four-wheelers. But they didn't move quickly enough, and Vince lined up on the driver of the pickup and two others who were unfortunate enough to be standing close by.

Flames and sparks leapt out of the end of his shotgun as the fifteen steel balls left the barrel. The three looters in their path didn't stand a chance at that range and were thrown to the ground by the force of the impact. One of them bounced off the side of the pickup before landing lifelessly on the ground, leaving a bloody stain and a dent where he hit the truck. The driver fell into the open door of the truck and clawed at the wheel for a moment before losing his grip and sliding down to the pavement in a hunched-over bloody mess.

Without hesitation, Vince pumped another round into the shotgun and lined up to take another shot. But everyone was moving now — and fast. The element of surprise was gone and he was now a target. A shot ricocheted off the concrete block wall in front of him and he dropped into a prone position behind the wall before he could get a shot off. From behind his cover, he heard gunshots and some of the ATVs revving up. A few of the shots landed dangerously close, as they hit the block wall in front of Vince. His mind flashed back to a time when he shot an old cinderblock with his .308. It took him only three rounds with the M1A to completely demolish the thing, and he was surprised at how fragile it was. He couldn't help but wonder how safe he really was.

Already lying flat on the roof, he rolled to his left, several feet down the wall, and popped up. He scanned the area, searching for a target, and caught a glimpse of someone hiding behind a thin metal sign at the edge of the property. The shooter had his gun trained where Vince had been when he took the first shot. The man saw Vince and began to turn his gun, but it was too late.

Vince squeezed the trigger and felt the kick of the gun as he launched another barrage of steel balls at his attacker. The distance was greater than the last shot, but even at forty yards, the steel tore through the thin aluminum sign like it was paper. The sheet metal rippled as the shot made contact and went through, leaving several holes behind. The man froze for a moment before dropping out of sight behind the advertisement.

Pumping another round into the chamber, Vince looked for his next target. The car directly below him came to life as the rear wheels chirped and began spinning their way through the broken glass from the back window. It began to pick up speed, moving backward through the parking lot and heading for the road. Vince unleashed another round of steel shots at the moving vehicle but misjudged. Sparks flew as the double-aught buck cut into the hood of the car, leaving behind a handful of small holes.

He tried to calm down as he searched for any immediate threats. The intruders were scattered now and a few of them were moving down the road on the ATVs.

He thought about taking another crack at the car, but it was out on the street now and he didn't want to waste another shot. With only three rounds left in the shotgun, he needed to save them in case there were any more looters still shooting at him. The car tires squealed as the driver cut the wheel and threw it in drive. Steam rose from the grill, and Vince was at least glad he'd done some damage to the vehicle.

The Ford pickup was still there, but then again, so was the driver. There were also a couple ATVs still parked in the lot, but those must have belonged to the bodies lying on the ground. Some of the gang who fled the scene early had doubled up on the ATVs and made their escape that way.

Vince crouched down behind the wall once again and surveyed the area. He still had to be careful. The recent breeze that kicked up during the skirmish was gone and the smoke was beginning to settle back in, obscuring his view. He couldn't see the motel parking lot or the van anymore and had no idea how Bill and Jim had made out. Vince thought about how much more damage he could have done if Jim hadn't blown it for them.

What was the guy thinking, running across the parking lot and shooting like a wild man? Jim was lucky he and Bill were prepared to help or else he would have been gunned down instantly. Not everybody could keep it together when faced with a situation like this. It wasn't that Jim was a danger per se, just that he probably couldn't be relied upon to follow through with a plan, especially if his actions today were his idea of a well-thought-out approach. Vince made a mental note to consider Jim a liability the next time they faced off with these people. And Vince was certain there would be a next time.

Sure, they had the upper hand this time and they had the advantage right now. The intruders had no idea how many of them there were, and that was good. They had fired on the gang from a few directions and surprised them. But now they knew what to expect, and when they came back, they'd be ready for a fight.

Their performance today had only bought them some time. How much time, though, Vince didn't know. The looters would go back and lick their wounds, only to return with revenge on their minds. With their leader down, Vince hoped it would take some time for them to regroup. The looters were down but far from out.

Based on Jim's description, there were more than what had shown up tonight. But how many more? There were easily a dozen people here tonight, but only one car and one truck. Jim said there were three cars and two trucks when he saw them earlier. They could have been the ones on the ATVs, but Vince doubted that. They wouldn't bring four-wheelers if they had other larger vehicles at their disposal to help empty out the store.

The rest of the gang was probably off looting somewhere else. There would still be other places with supplies if they hadn't burned down. But those resources wouldn't last long. Once the looters had exhausted the easy targets, they'd be back. Vince gathered his .45 and the box of shotgun shells. Satisfied the threat had passed, he started for the ladder.

"Major, come quick," Bill called out from somewhere off in the distance.

Vince could tell by the sound of Bill's voice that something was wrong. "Hang on. I'm on my way."

· 24 ·

Vince tucked the .45 into the holster and descended the ladder as fast as he could while juggling the shotgun and the box of ammo. As he came out of the rear yard and exited the gate, he glanced over at the Ford pickup and the bodies on the ground around it. Between the lack of movement and the pools of blood they were lying in, it was safe to assume they were dead. But as badly as he wanted to get to Bill, he had to make sure.

He thought about gathering their weapons, but his hands were already full. He'd come back later with some help and gets things squared away. Careful not to put his foot in the expanding pool of blood, he stepped over the body and checked out the inside the Ford. It was mostly empty except for the floor, which was littered with empty beer cans and trash. He was glad to see the keys dangling from the ignition and reached in to grab them.

Another running vehicle would be a huge help to them, especially since the van was a loss and wouldn't be drivable the way it was.

"Vince, hurry!" Bill called out again.

"I'm coming." Vince shoved the keys in his pocket and jogged over to where the man had been hiding behind the sign. He was dead as well. The lifeless body lay in the fetal position on the ground, his hand still clutching the AR-15 that he shot at Vince with. Vince kicked at the gun until it broke free of the man's stiff dead hand and skittered across the pavement a few feet. Satisfied there were no more threats, Vince continued toward the motel and the sound of Bill's voice.

On the way out of the parking lot, he noticed a trail of antifreeze on the ground, which led out to the road and followed the path the car had taken while making its hasty escape from the shootout. If only he'd aimed a little higher, they wouldn't have gotten away.

As he crossed the road, he could see flashlights through the smoke. It looked like everyone was outside and standing around in a circle. No one was talking and they were all looking down at the ground. Vince slowed to a walk as he approached and tried to catch his breath. He was glad to see Cy safe and standing among the small group.

"What's going on?" Vince asked. Only a few of them looked back in his direction.

Cy shook his head. "It's Jim."

Vince approached as the others stepped aside to reveal Reese kneeling over Jim's body. She held a blood-stained wad of gauze on his neck as she turned to look at Vince with watery eyes. She shook her head slowly, got up from her knees, and took a few steps back, her hands covered in Jim's blood. He'd taken a direct hit to the neck and bled out on the ground. There was nothing any of them could have done for him.

They stood around in silence for what felt like a couple minutes while they processed what happened. Fred put his hand on his daughter's shoulder and pulled her back even farther.

"There was nothing you could do, honey. It's okay," Hannah said through a cough. She was right. Judging by the location of the wound and the amount of blood on the ground, Jim most likely died in a matter of seconds after he was hit. Reese's parents led her away and headed back toward the motel while the others stood fast.

"Hold these." Vince handed the box of ammo and the shotgun to Cy before crouching down by the body. He ran his fingers over Jim's still open eyes and closed them before moving his feet together.

"Tom, give me a hand, will you?" Vince asked. "We can't leave him out here."

"Sure." Tom bent down and grabbed his arms.

Jim's head fell back as they lifted him off the ground, exposing the large hole in his neck. Vince looked away but the image was burned into his mind. He hadn't seen a wound like that in a long time, and it brought back memories of things he'd rather forget.

"Get the gun." Vince looked at Bill, who was as still as a statue and rather pale. Bill didn't answer and instead nodded slowly. Using only a couple fingers to avoid getting bloody, he carefully picked the oversized revolver up off the ground. Bill had probably seen Jim get hit, and judging by the carnage, it had left an impression on the man. Bill was a good mechanic and, as far as Vince knew, a standup guy, but this was something he wasn't prepared for. Vince had to remind himself that not everyone was equipped to deal with things like this.

Unfortunately, this was the new world in which they lived, and there were tougher days ahead. As they carried Jim's body around the side of the building, Vince couldn't help but think that they had just lost an able-bodied person who could have helped out with a lot of things. They were going to need everyone if they were going to survive, and this was a big loss, even if Jim was a little impulsive. Vince felt guilty for thinking the things that went through his mind earlier when he dismissed him as a liability.

There were only twelve of them now, two of whom were young children. That wasn't many people, considering the amount of work that lay ahead. Hopefully they would find more survivors after the fires died down. It was a catch-22, though, and more people needed more supplies. They would all have to pull their weight to survive. There was no room for those who didn't want to work or help out in any way they could. Even those with physical limitations would have to find a way to contribute to the overall cause. It was harsh, but it was the way it had to be.

Mary, a folded sheet in her hands, appeared from around the corner of the building. "We should cover him," she said.

Vince took the sheet from her and unfurled it over Jim's body. He and Tom wrapped the body up before carrying it the last couple feet to the edge of the property and out of sight of the others.

"We tried to stop him but he wouldn't listen," Tom said.

"He thought you and Bill were in trouble. He wanted to help," Mary added. The words stung, and Vince couldn't help but feel partly responsible for Jim's death. What Mary said only added to the feeling of guilt he already struggled with.

As the three of them returned to the motel, Vince tried to put it out of his mind. It wasn't the first time he'd lost a man and been haunted by the feeling that he could have done something differently to prevent a tragedy. But right now, there were bigger issues to deal with, and he had the rest of his life to feel bad about what happened to Jim. Now they had to stay focused and capitalize on their slight advantage over the intruders. They needed to prepare themselves as best as they could for the next attack. It wasn't a matter of *if*—it was a matter of *when*. It wasn't just the supplies in the garage the looters would be after next time either. Next time, they would be looking for something far more sinister: revenge. Suddenly, the smoke and fires seemed like the least of Vince's concerns.

· 25 ·

Vince had everyone gather in the back room of the motel, where they normally served the continental breakfast for guests. Once he had everyone, except for the children and Beverly, who had volunteered to stay with them back at the room, he called the meeting to order.

Vince went over some of his concerns and what he thought were priorities crucial to their survival. He outlined a rough plan of attack for after the fires died down and the smoke cleared. Unfortunately, there was no point in venturing out until that happened. With the limited medical supplies they managed to save, they couldn't afford to have anyone else get hurt or risk smoke inhalation.

Reese had come up with a written inventory of what they had. She cautioned that they would need every bit of it to treat any survivors they found after the fires, and she was right. She had also procured potassium iodine pills in their haul from the pharmacy and passed them out to everyone, just in case they had been exposed to radiation from the nukes. Vince had his doubts about whether they would do any good, but he kept them to himself. If nothing else they were worth it to maintain morale.

To Vince's surprise, everyone agreed with his priorities. He expected at least some resistance or differing opinions, but they all seemed glad to let him take charge and lay out a plan. He wasn't sure if it was genuine or because some of them were still in a state of shock and denial about what was happening around them. The responsibility of being in charge wasn't a job he wanted, but someone had to keep things moving, and these people looked up to him whether he liked it or not. It was a big responsibility, and he promised to do his best not to let them down.

The first order of business was getting the power back up and running at the garage. If he could manage that, they would have access to clean, drinkable water. He and Cy would go back over to the garage and see if they could restore power while the others stayed at the motel and out of the smoke for the time being.

He didn't mention it to the others, but they would also gather weapons from the dead gang members. He didn't want Cy to have any illusions about what was going on. It wasn't something he particularly wanted his son to be a part of, but he also wanted Cy to see things for how they were. The sooner Cy realized that this was survival of the fittest, the more prepared he would be for what lay ahead.

Before they headed across the street, Vince wanted to do something to prepare for the smoke they would be exposed to. He'd breathed enough of it in already and didn't want to push his luck and trigger any health problems. His throat was already hoarse and irritated; spending more time outside would only make things worse, and the paper hardware masks weren't cutting it.

As the others headed back to their rooms, Vince asked Cy to stay behind.

"Come with me," Vince said.

"What are we doing? I thought we were going over to the garage," Cy asked.

"We are, but first I want to make a couple masks for us. I don't want to breathe in any more of that smoke. We've done enough of that today."

Cy followed his dad into the small kitchen area of the motel and began to look around the room. "What are we looking for?" Cy asked.

"We need a couple empty containers big enough to fit over our faces." Vince found a closet filled with cleaning supplies. It had a few containers that might work, but he quickly dismissed that idea and ruled them out. Breathing out of something that held a cleaning agent wasn't a great idea and would probably do more damage than the smoke itself.

"What about these?" Cy held up a couple of clear plastic two-liter juice bottles that he pulled out of a recycling bin.

"Perfect." Vince grabbed some new cleaning sponges and a roll of duct tape from the supply closet and met Cy at the stainless-steel workstation in the middle of the kitchen. He pulled his knife from his pocket and began working on the bottles, cutting the bottoms and part of the backs of both bottles off in a pattern so they would fit around their faces. Vince held the bottle up to his face several times, testing the fit until he was satisfied.

"Let me see your mask," Vince said.

Cy pulled the paper mask from around his neck and handed it to his dad, then watched as Vince began to take it apart. He cut small slits into the first bottle and used the elastic from the mask to make a head strap, then reinforced it with the duct tape. He then wrapped the roughly cut edge of the bottle with duct tape to soften it and provide a better seal.

"Take these and get them wet with the melted ice from the freezer." Vince handed the sponges to Cy. As Cy soaked the sponges, Vince continued working on the other bottle. By the time Cy returned with two wet sponges, the masks were almost ready. Vince shoved the sponges into the necks of the bottles until they pushed up against the lids. He unscrewed the bottle top and put one of the makeshift masks on. He inhaled slowly through the device and gave Cy a thumbs-up. It took a little work to get a full breath through the small opening and it smelled like old apple juice and stale water, but it was better than breathing in smoke that contained God knew what kind of carcinogens.

"Try yours," Vince said. Cy put the strange-looking mask over his face and took a deep breath. The plastic crinkled and popped as it conformed to his face with each inhalation. Cy nodded and returned the thumbs-up signal. The masks weren't pretty, but they would do the trick.

On their way out of the motel, Vince stopped and checked the desk drawers in the office behind the front counter. He was looking for a box of ammo that Jim might have stashed somewhere.

"Check behind the front desk and see if you can find any ammo for Jim's pistol, will you?" Vince asked.

"Sure," Cy said. But before Cy could even begin looking, Vince spotted a red and black box of .44 Rem Mag soft points in the back of the top drawer. He grabbed the heavy box and looked inside. He was glad to see the box of fifty was mostly full.

After they carried Jim's body around back, Vince asked Bill to give the handgun to Tom. Bill was still visibly shaken from the gunfight. Vince took Bill's truck keys and sent him back to his room to be with his wife and daughter and, hopefully, pull himself together. Tom needed a weapon, and Bill already had his rifle, so it made sense to give Tom the handgun. He briefly considered letting Mary have the gun, but the .44-caliber pistol would kick like a mule. As tough as she was, he wasn't sure Mary could handle it with any accuracy. In talking with Tom, Vince learned that he was in the navy for several years and was also a hunter. He felt better about him having the miniature hand cannon.

Vince and Cy made their way out of the motel lobby and into the smoke. They donned their makeshift masks and tried them out.

"Is yours working?" Vince shouted through the plastic.

Cy nodded and gave him a thumbs-up.

"Wait here a sec." Vince hurried over to the room that Tom and his family were staying in and was glad to see Tom keeping watch at the window. Vince had asked him to take the first shift of what would be an around-the-clock lookout.

Having someone awake and on lookout was one of the things he had proposed at the meeting and another reason for Tom to have the pistol. If Tom saw anything or anyone coming down the road, he was to step outside the room and fire one shot in the air as a warning.

Tom saw Vince coming and opened the door to let him in, but Vince was in a hurry and handed him the box of ammo for the pistol and started to leave without saying anything.

"Major," Tom said.

Vince stopped and turned to face him. "What is it?"

"The van. It's in the way. I can't see very well," Tom explained.

Vince nodded. "I'll take care of it." Tom began to cough as he retreated into the room and shut the door. The smoke was still bad, and Vince was glad he'd taken the time to make the masks for him and Cy.

Vince got Cy's attention and pointed to the van. The two met at the battered old Chevy, which still sat where Fred and Hannah had ground to a halt earlier. Vince was happy to see the keys still in the ignition and even more pleased to hear the engine roar to life as he slid into the driver's seat. The left front tire was missing, leaving only a badly bent rim. But the van was rear-wheel drive, and if he kept it in reverse, they should be able to make it across the street and to the garage without too much trouble.

Moving the van to the garage was something he planned on doing eventually. He was sure he could find a wheel that fit the van and get it back up and running. Even with the bad transmission, it would be handy for hauling supplies. He hadn't planned on fooling with it now, but it was in the way, and if moving it would give Tom a better view of the road, then it was worth doing now. The last thing Vince wanted was the looters to surprise him while he and Cy were trying to restore the power inside the shop.

· 26 ·

Cy climbed into the passenger's seat and was about to close the door when Vince stopped him.

"You might want to leave that open. I'm going to need you to keep an eye out as we back up and make sure I don't run into anything," Vince said. It was hard enough to see with all the smoke in the air, but the van's rear windows and side mirrors had been charred black with soot from Fred and Hannah's close call with the fires, making it impossible to see behind them.

Cy hung on to the door as he looked behind the van and Vince put it in gear. The wheel lurched in his hand as he struggled to keep it steady, the front rim cutting into the pavement as they began to move backward.

"Curb!" Cy yelled out as the van bounced off the sidewalk and into the street. Luckily, the garage was a fairly straight shot across the street and the gate to the rear yard was directly behind them.

Slowly but surely, they progressed across the street, the front rim resisting the entire way and making loud grinding noises as they went. Judging by how the van was handling, Vince wasn't sure the front wheel without the tire was even turning anymore. He wrestled the wheel and tried to keep it as straight as possible. The rear wheels chirped and spun occasionally as they dragged the van backward. Vince struggled to keep between the two sides of the gate, but the van drifted to the right, forcing Cy to close his door as the chain-link gate scraped down the side of the van and tore the mirror off his door.

"Sorry," Vince said, but there was nothing he could do about it as the rim dug into the gravel and dirt, forcing them to the side and leaving a small trench in their wake. Satisfied the van was far enough into the rear yard and out of the way for the time being, he turned it off and left the keys in the ignition.

"Good enough," Vince said.

Out of habit, Vince hopped out of the van and headed for the rear door of his shop before remembering that it was damaged in the attempted break-in that morning.

"We'll have to use the front door."

Cy followed him back through the gate and around to the front, where the Ford pickup was parked next to Bill's truck.

"We need to gather up the guns and bring them inside." Vince headed over to the body behind the sign and the gun he had kicked away from the man earlier while Cy gathered the weapons from around the pickup. When Vince returned, his son was standing over the bodies and staring at the pool of blood that surrounded them.

"Come on. Let's get inside," Vince said. Cy remained silent as he stepped away and followed his dad inside the building.

They laid the weapons on the front counter and took stock of what they had: two shotguns and an AR-15. Vince had hoped to score a few rifles. They were covered in the close-range department and could have used more weapons capable of shooting longer distances. With the current visibility outside, that didn't matter right now, but it would when the smoke cleared.

The shotguns were both 12-gauges, and that much was good. The box of shells Vince had would work in both. When he divided the ammo among the three shotguns, though, there wasn't much to go around. The AR was chambered in .223, and the thirty-round magazine felt about half-full, the missing bullets lodged in the concrete wall he hid behind during the fight. With any luck, they'd find more ammo in the Ford pickup. The additional guns were a great find, but without ammo, they were useless.

"Sorry." Cy cringed and dialed it back until the lamp emitted a soft dull glow.

"There you go. That'll do." Vince, anxious to stop advertising their presence to the outside world, led them toward the back of the building. The two made their way into the shelf-lined storage room at the rear of the garage. The shelves were filled with boxes of car parts that would now most likely never be used. Along the far-left wall, blocking access to the panel box and the DC to AC current inverter, were several empty propane tanks waiting to be filled and put in front of the store.

Vince operated a propane refill station at his garage, most commonly used for the twenty-pound tanks found on barbecue grills and also the larger tanks on board RVs. The camping season hadn't really kicked off yet, and the large thousand-gallon propane storage tank he drew from out back in the yard was close to full.

If he couldn't get the power on, that gas would provide all they needed for cooking and light and maybe even heat if all this lasted into the winter. But he was getting ahead of himself. There was no point in worrying about any of that now. Their main concern was surviving the night.

· 27 ·

Cy set the lantern down on a worktable in the center of the room and joined his dad, who had already started moving the empty gas tanks away from the wall and the electrical boxes. Neither of them spoke much, but that was okay with Cy. He had plenty on his mind, not the least of which was his mother back in Washington and his ex-girlfriend, Kate.

He and Kate split up less than a month ago, and it was a less-than-pleasant parting of the ways. They had been together for over two years, and breaking up was hard and complicated but the right thing to do. She had become controlling and increasingly unhappy about his recent interest in joining the army. He had hoped to talk to his dad about it on his trip to Indiana this summer, a conversation that seemed pointless now.

His job at the motorcycle shop back home wasn't

cutting it and left him feeling unsatisfied at the end of the day. He felt like it was a dead end with no chance for advancement. He began to consider a career in the military and thought maybe the army would be a good fit. After all, his dad had done pretty well for himself and retired at a young age. His girlfriend, however, wasn't the least bit thrilled with the idea of him running off and joining the army, and it became the source of countless arguments.

Still, for all the fighting and animosity between them, he still loved her and was worried about her well-being. She had family in the area with a farm outside Olympia, and he hoped she survived the initial attack and was safe with them.

He had good reason to believe she was okay. Kate wasn't your typical girly-girl, and with two older brothers and a father who were all avid outdoorsman, she had grown up a tomboy. Kate had a can-do attitude and wasn't afraid to get her hands dirty. They spent a lot of their free time backpacking and hiking around Mt. Rainer National Park with her husky, Kenai. That dog was a light sleeper and very vocal about any noises he heard during the night around Kate's apartment complex. There was no way Kenai would let her sleep through the EMP detonations. Another thing that gave him reason to hope was that she drove an '82 Jeep CJ-7. She would have been able to drive to her family's property outside of the city and get away from the dangers there.

"Hey, turn that up a little, will you?" Vince asked, looking at the lantern. His dad had the panel box open and was looking over the breakers. Cy had drifted off in thought and hadn't realized how dim it was in there. He nodded and turned the gas feed up until the light filled the room.

"It should be okay to use the light back here. No one will be able to see it from out front," his dad assured him.

But Cy was deep in thought again, this time about his mother. She was the exact opposite of Kate—and his dad, for that matter. Cy wasn't as optimistic about her well-being. His mom was a big-time real estate agent in her own right and an even bigger socialite around Seattle. Her Sunday morning routine consisted of sleeping in and recovering from a busy weekend of parties or social events. She was a heavy sleeper and far from a morning person.

This past winter, he had a pipe break in his apartment, which caused a small flood and forced him to move out temporarily. He ended up staying with his mom for a few days while the repairs were done at his place. Tiptoeing around in the mornings got old fast, but it was better than the alternative of waking her up and subjecting himself to a mini-lecture about how she needed her rest and how not everyone was up and running by seven in the morning. Cy knew the chances of his mother waking up early today and escaping the high-rise luxury apartment building where she lived was very unlikely.

Still, though, he hung on to the hope that the noise of the detonations woke her up and she had made it out of the building. Or maybe the building survived the EMP pulse and remained intact. But he couldn't help thinking about the high-rises in Indianapolis and how they weathered the blast. There wasn't a single building that looked unaffected by the bombs. The image of shattered windows and burning buildings flashed through his mind as he tried to put it out of his thoughts.

Maybe Seattle hadn't been hit. Maybe she was okay. But no matter how much he tried to convince himself that his mother was all right, he knew otherwise in his gut.

"Cy, are you okay?" His dad caught him off guard with the question.

"What? Oh yeah, I was just thinking...about Mom and Kate. Do you think they're okay?" he asked.

His dad stopped flipping breaker switches and turned to look at Cy, his expression changing. "I don't know." Vince sighed. "It depends how hard Seattle was hit. It may not have been a target at all. Maybe they're in better shape than we are. From what you've told me about Kate, she seems like she can take care of herself. You told me she drives an old Jeep, so she'd be able to make it out to her family's place."

Cy nodded as his dad turned his attention back to the panel box and began flipping breakers off again. His dad hadn't really addressed his concerns about his mother, which told Cy all he needed to know.

"All right, here goes nothing." *Click*. Vince threw a larger red switch between the electrical panel for the garage and the power inverter. Cy heard a distinct humming noise, and for a moment, he forgot about his troubles.

"See if you can get water out of the tap at the sink in the garage bay." His dad tossed him the flashlight.

"Really?" Cy asked.

"Yeah, I've got everything turned off but the well pump. There should be enough solar power stored in the backup batteries to run the pump for a little while."

Cy left the storage room and turned the flashlight on. He found the deep sink in the far corner of the garage bay and twisted the knob on the faucet. The faucet hissed and spat for a few seconds as he waited impatiently. Finally, he was rewarded with a slow but steady stream of water. He stuck his hands into the cool fresh water as it poured out of the tap, then brought a few handfuls up to his face. At that moment, nothing else mattered but the relief the water brought to his dirty, grit-encrusted face. He put his mouth to the faucet and took several large swallows of the clean water before thinking to call out to his dad.

"It's working!" he yelled between gulps and noticed that his throat didn't hurt when he talked anymore.

"Good. We'll fill some containers and take it to the others," his dad said.

When he had his fill, Cy turned the water off and grabbed a paper towel from the nearby dispenser to dry his face and hands. For the first time since they'd seen the EMPs detonate in Indianapolis, he felt like there was a chance that everything would be okay. Of course, *okay* meant something entirely different today than it had yesterday.

· 28 ·

Vince was relieved that the batteries had enough juice to run the well pump. They were lucky the circuit breaker had tripped and done its job when the EMP pulse hit. He wasn't planning on taking any chances, though, and after they filled the containers of water to take back with them, he planned to throw the breaker again. He was careful to turn off all the breakers in the panel box to the exterior lights and anything nonessential. But even if there wasn't anything on, the power would still drain out of the batteries. And with the skies filled with smoke, there was no telling how long they'd take to recharge.

Vince and Cy set about filling four of the large water storage containers that he sold with the camping gear in his store. They worked as fast as they could so they didn't waste any of the power in the reserve batteries. There was a good chance they might need power again to retrieve more water before they saw sunlight and the solar panels could recharge the batteries.

He realized then that adding more batteries to the system to store the DC power from the solar panels would be important. Something else on his growing list of things to do. Car batteries would be the easiest and most available things to use. Most of the cars that were running seemed to have caught on fire, but he noticed several parked vehicles around town that looked intact—at least the ones that hadn't been parked too close to any burning buildings.

If he could get enough car batteries and link them all together, they could store enough power to have a couple hours' worth of utilities—enough to supply the motel rooms with electricity and running water for at least a couple hours per night if everyone agreed to conserve and limit their usage. Having water and power would be huge, and it would keep everyone's morale up, which would be hard to do, given the dire circumstances.

Vince knew firsthand how the lack of basic creature comforts could tear a person down and rob them of the will to live or, at the very least, keep them from exerting any effort to survive. And there was going to be a great deal of effort needed in the coming days and weeks. He would need everyone chipping in and doing their share if they were going to make it. And he wanted to do more than just get by—not so much for himself, but for Cy and Reese and the other kids.

It would be a long time before things returned to normal, and Vince doubted it would ever really be the same as it was. He felt guilty for his next thought, but maybe this was what the country needed in some ways. A hard reset.

In his opinion, the country had moved far from center, and politics had become increasingly divisive over the last couple decades or so. No one listened anymore, and it was all about who could shout the loudest and cry victim in the most convincing way. Special interest groups were running the country and shaping policy more than the elected officials. Vince couldn't think of a single member of Congress or the Senate who he thought truly represented the people. The presidential elections over the last several cycles seemed more like schoolyard fights between two bullies. No matter who won, you were still going to lose your lunch money.

As far as he was concerned, the last good man for the job was Ronald Reagan, but they didn't make them like that anymore. The kids growing up today were rewarded for mediocrity, and it was producing a generation of entitlement. Even if another Reagan were to come along, Vince wasn't so sure he could accomplish anything in the current political climate. Even the media had chosen sides and wasn't afraid to show their biases. Vince remembered when you could watch the news at night and get straightforward facts about events and decide for yourself. But those days were long gone, and facts no longer carried as much weight as feelings did. The line between news and so-called comedians on the late-night talk shows was so blurred at this point that it was hard to tell the difference. Bipartisanship was dead, and it was all about who could drag the other more deeply through the mud.

But none of that mattered anymore. For better or for worse, this was the beginning of a new era in this country, and they had no choice in the matter. Vince had a saying he liked to use when customers would stop by the garage and see their beloved vehicle in parts and pieces on the shop floor. He would tell them, "You've got to break a few eggs to make an omelet." And it was safe to say all the eggs were broken now. That statement usually got a few nervous chuckles out of the customer, but there was nothing to laugh about now. It was true, though; things always looked their worst before getting better.

They had to remain hopeful. Otherwise, what was the point to all this? Vince had to believe there was a future for the kids and even him. As screwed up as the government was, the survivors would surely rise from the ashes and rebuild. Eventually, they would see the National Guard or FEMA camps for the survivors, although he was less excited about the latter. The question was, how long would it take before the common person was a priority for the government? Surely, it was in self-preservation mode right now and scrambling all available assets. Without communication, that would be tough. It could be weeks, months, or maybe even years before they got any help.

Vince remembered reading recently about the military's efforts regarding EMP preparedness over the last few years. There were budget battles, and as usual, the wheels of progress moved slowly. But supposedly the military was beginning to implement some plans in case of an EMP attack and had begun to outfit equipment and vehicles for just such a scenario. Of course, he had no idea how far they had gotten or to what extent they were prepared.

From what Vince knew about EMPs, there was a lot of speculation on what would actually happen after multiple detonations. How far the pulse reached and the extent of damage largely depended on several factors. Two things that were mentioned in just about every article he read were the size of the bomb and the altitude at which it was detonated.

He was pretty sure what they had witnessed in Indianapolis was an HEMP or a high-altitude EMP. The higher the altitude, the bigger the affected area.

Or so the theory said. In reality, it was better than a traditional nuclear weapon. If it had been a large detonation at ground level, they wouldn't be here right now. Not that what had happened was good by any stretch of the imagination, but at least it wasn't game over. Far from it, in fact, if Vince had any say in the matter.

As he and Cy loaded the last of the bright blue five-gallon water containers into the back of Bill's Dodge, neither mentioned the bodies that lay on the ground by the Ford pickup. Vince sent Cy in to gather the guns they collected while Vince considered what to do. Part of him wanted to let them be and deal with it later, but it needed to be done sooner rather than later. In this heat, the task wasn't going to get any more pleasant. It was best to get it over with.

Cy exited the store, juggling an armful of guns and wearing his mask again, while Vince locked the door behind him, although he wasn't sure why. It wasn't like it would stop anyone from accessing to the store. The gang of looters would think nothing of smashing the windows and taking what they wanted when they returned.

"You up to helping me move the bodies?" Vince positioned his mask back over his face.

"Yeah, I guess so." Cy exhaled loudly as he unloaded the weapons into the bed of Bill's truck and closed the tailgate.

"Let's use the Ford," Vince said.

"Where are we taking them?" Cy asked.

"Let's take them around the outside of the fence to the back of the property." Out of sight would be best, and later, if they found a piece of equipment, he could dig a hole in the field behind the garage and bury the bodies.

Careful and trying not to get any blood on themselves, they loaded the stiffening corpses one by one onto the tailgate of the Ford. Once they had them loaded, they got into the truck. Cy pushed the empty beer cans and trash out of his way with his feet as he sat in the passenger's seat.

"What a mess."

"Yeah, but not really a surprise, considering the people. Hey, check in the glovebox, will you?" Vince asked.

Cy popped open the small compartment. "Ammo!"

Vince leaned over and saw two boxes of shotgun shells. One was birdshot and the other was a smaller box of rifled deer slugs.

"Are they full?" Vince asked.

Cy opened both boxes and inspected them. "A little more than half a box of the number 3 bird load and all ten of the slugs."

"Good. We'll need 'em." He was hoping for more assault rifle ammo, but this was better than nothing. The number 3 load would only be good for close range and probably wasn't lethal to a human beyond twenty yards, but it would be a strong deterrent at least. The rifled slugs normally used for deer hunting were the real find. Although neither shotgun they had acquired looked to have a rifled barrel, the slugs would be much more accurate at longer ranges. Even in a shotgun with a smooth-bore barrel, the slugs would be accurate from seventy-five to a hundred yards out. It was the best thing they had next to the AR-15 and Bill's hunting rifle.

Vince fired up the old Ford and put it into gear. He pulled around to the far side of the lot and backed the truck up along the outside fence line of his vehicle storage yard.

"Hang on." Vince sped up as they neared the edge of the wheat field and then hit the brakes hard once they were over the property line and into the tall grass. The truck came to an abrupt stop as all but one of the bodies tumbled off the tailgate with a sickening thud.

"Wait here. I got it." Vince threw the truck in gear and hopped out. Wading through the taller grass, he made his way to the rear of the truck and grabbed the pant leg of the remaining body. It didn't take much effort to pull it out. He considered checking for ammo they might have been carrying but decided against it. He was tired of looking at them and just wanted to bring the water to the others. He closed the tailgate and joined Cy in the truck.

"Are we just going to leave them there?" Cy asked.

"For now. We'll bury them later." Vince hoped Cy didn't think he was being too cold-hearted, but there was no time for that. Besides, those lowlifes didn't deserve any more of their time. The others needed water, and Vince needed to get back and come up with a plan.

· 29 ·

Vince dropped Cy off at Bill's truck and handed him the keys. In the trucks, the two headed back to the motel, and for the first time that day, Vince felt like they were making progress and had actually accomplished something besides managing to stay alive. He also realized just how physically and mentally exhausted he was. Even the hard and cracked vinyl seats in the pickup truck felt good right now, and he appreciated the chance to sit, even if it was only for the short time it took to drive across the street.

He was hungry and a little dehydrated, but he was sure he wasn't alone in that. The others felt the same, he was sure. He didn't carry much food in the store, but he did have the typical convenience store selection of snacks and candy on the shelves and a glass-front cooler filled with soda and sports drinks. He and Cy grabbed a small assortment of snacks and sports drinks to take back to the others as they were loading up.

It was Cy's idea, and it was a good one. They would have to ration what food they had, but tonight was an exception. They had all been through a lot today, and as far as Vince knew, none of them had had anything to eat and very little to drink. What they gathered from the store wouldn't make much of a meal, but it would be much appreciated. Besides, he needed everyone to get a good night's sleep. Tomorrow would be a big day that would surely test their limits.

Vince had multiple ideas and plans in his head. All would take a lot of manpower to accomplish. He would need every able-bodied person to be ready to work tomorrow. Of course, all this depended on the fires dying down and the smoke thinning out enough to see and breathe. He could rig up some more masks, but they weren't that comfortable and tended to fog up quickly in this heat. Getting anything done while wearing them would be tough at best, and struggling to draw a full breath would be counterproductive. Most of them had breathed in enough smoke already.

He didn't want to admit it, but getting anything done tomorrow might be wishful thinking on his part. If it didn't clear up, they might have to wait it out from the relative safety of their motel rooms. Vince didn't have a lot of patience, and waiting it out would be harder for him than getting out and working on one of the many ideas bouncing around his head.

Waiting also meant time to dwell on things, something he thought wasn't good for anybody right now. Staying busy was the best way to keep your mind out of the gutter—at least, it was for him. Too much time with nothing to do could really bring down a person's morale in times of hardship. But there was nothing he could do about it except wait and see what tomorrow brought.

With any luck, the intruders wouldn't return tonight and Vince and the others could all get some much-needed rest. Someone would have to stand watch at all times, and they needed to set up a schedule. Tom was on lookout duty now, and if he was up for it, Vince would ask him to stick with it until midnight. A four-hour rotating shift would be best, and even if there were only a handful of people in the rotation, that would allow for a lot of time off between a person's watch duties.

This was going to be a new way of life from here on out, and Vince hoped they were all up to the challenge. Of course, he doubted any of them expected anything less than a drastic change from the norm. But still, he was sure disagreements about how to do things would arise and he wasn't opposed to ideas from any of them. If someone wanted to step up and take charge of a task, he wasn't going to stop them as long as it was for the good of the group.

Vince pulled into the motel parking lot and swung the pickup around so he could back in and be close to the rooms. He turned the truck off and gave two short blasts on the horn before getting out. Cy backed the big Dodge in next to him, then joined his dad at the tailgate, where they started going through the supplies they brought back.

"Hey, Dad?"

"Yeah?"

"Do you think it would be okay if I took the room next to ours? The bed is a little small, and no offense, but you snore like a chainsaw." Cy cracked a smile that was visible through the fogged-up mask.

Vince laughed. "Yeah, I don't see why not." He was glad to see that Cy still had a sense of humor after the trials of the day. They might as well spread out and have their own beds. There was no telling how long they would have that luxury. It all depended on how many people ended up living at the motel. Vince hoped they would find enough survivors to fill the place. Although that would mean a lot of mouths to feed, there was safety in numbers and it would make their lives easier in the long run.

The others began to file out of their rooms and gather at the back of the truck while Vince and Cy divided up the food and water into equal piles.

"I'll keep this short so you can all get back inside and out of this smoke." Vince turned to face the small group and leaned on the truck. Cy finished up what he was doing and stopped to listen.

"I know it's not much, but it will have to do until tomorrow. Divide it up among yourselves, and everyone take a five-gallon container of water for their room. We all need to get a good night's rest and hopefully tomorrow we can try to get organized a little. Someone is going to have to stay up and keep an eye out for those guys in case they come back. Tom, can you stay at it until midnight?" Vince asked.

"Yeah, no problem," Tom said.

"Bill, can you relive Tom at twelve? We'll take four-hour shifts around the clock, me included." Vince started to take off his watch to give to Tom.

"I got it. Bev's watch is still working. I can use that," Tom said.

"Good, everyone is in charge of waking up their relief," Vince added.

"What do we do if they come back?" Hannah asked while trying to hold back a cough.

"We fight. That's our only choice. We have a couple extra guns and some ammo." Vince reached into the truck and grabbed the two shotguns. He handed one to Fred and one to Mary.

"Mary, I know you know how to handle that. What about you, Fred?"

Fred looked the gun over. "I can handle it."

"Bill, you've got your rifle. Cy, I want you to take the AR-15. We don't have a lot of ammo, so when the time comes, use it wisely. If I can get to my house in the next day or so, I can add to our arsenal with both guns and ammo." Vince looked around at everyone. They were all tired and beat down, most of them coughing occasionally.

"All right. Let's get this stuff divided up and get back indoors," Vince added. Everyone moved to the tailgate and divvied up the food and drinks among themselves. A five-gallon container of water went to each room until only one remained. Vince took off his mask and handed it to Tom.

"Why don't you sit in the truck and keep watch from there. If you see anything, you can blow the horn." Vince walked around to the passenger's side and pulled out the two boxes of 12-gauge shells from the glovebox. He took three of the rifled slugs out from the ten-round box.

"Why don't you hang on to these? The birdshot won't do you any good if you have to cover any distance, but the slugs will give you at least seventy-five yards or so." Vince handed over the shells. Tom nodded and put them in his shirt pocket.

Vince planned on hanging on to the rest of the ammo for now since it was too scarce and too valuable to let out of his sight. He also planned on hanging on to the shortened shotgun from the garage. He still had his .45 but wasn't sure about handing out any more weapons at the moment.

Vince watched as everyone dispersed and went back to their rooms. They all moved like zombies as they shuffled away with their meager food allotment for the night. The looks on their soot- and dirt-encrusted faces told Vince everything he needed to know about how they were feeling. Was this really happening? What did it all mean for them? Their lives—or at least the lives they had known—were gone forever.

They were just as confused as he was about what was going on around them. Their world had been turned upside down and they were faced with the very real possibility of death at each and every turn. Even for those who had endured hardships before now, this was by far the worst thing they had ever seen. The future that each and every one of them had envisioned for themselves and for their children was gone, broken and shattered like their town, which lay in ruins around them.

· 30 ·

Tom took his place in the pickup and prepared to finish his watch shift while everyone disappeared into their rooms. Vince glanced at his watch and saw that it was almost 10:00 p.m. That surprised him, because he felt like it should have been much later. It was easy to lose track of time in the thick smoke.

He grabbed the remaining ammo and the shortened shotgun before heading to the room behind Mary. He spotted Cy talking to Reese outside the Morgans' room and asked him to bring the water to his and Mary's room when he came. Cy could get cleaned up in their room before heading next door. They had a few leftover empty water bottles that he could fill and have for himself later in the night if he wanted.

When Vince entered his and Mary's room, an overly enthusiastic Nugget greeted him by jumping from one bed to the other. Mary settled the little dog down and joined Nugget on the bed. Vince took a seat in one of the chairs and took off his boots. It felt good to let his feet breathe. He rubbed them for a while as he thought about all that he needed to do.

Cy pushed the door open with his foot as he lugged the heavy water container into the room and hoisted it up on the dresser in front of the TV. Mary didn't waste any time and grabbed a towel from the bathroom and wet it down with water.

"I'm going to get cleaned up as much as I can. Unless you want to go first?" she asked.

"No, you go right ahead," Vince said. He didn't mind. Besides, he had cleaned up a little with soap and water over at the garage. He felt bad about that now as Mary made do with the wet towel and headed into the bathroom with her flashlight.

"Are you still going to take the room next door?" Vince asked Cy.

"Yep, I already got the key." Cy twirled a room key around his finger a few times.

"Why don't you fill up those empty bottles for yourself?" Vince said.

"Good idea." Cy set about filling the bottles sitting on the nightstand. Vince moved the ammo to one of the dresser drawers and leaned the shotgun next to the bed, where he could reach it if he needed to. Next, he pulled the .45 and the holster from his waistband and laid it on the small table by the door. It felt good not to have it pressing into the small of his back anymore. He noticed Nugget watching his every move as he made his way about the room. Lying on the corner of the bed, the little dog waited impatiently for Mary to return.

Vince sat down at the edge of his bed and rubbed his eyes as he tried not to think about anything for a change. Cy finished filling the last water bottle. As he started for the door, he held them in his left arm and grabbed his AR-15 with the other.

"Well I guess I'll see you in the morning," Cy said, then let himself out of the room.

"Try to get some rest. Big day tomorrow. Goodnight," Vince said as the door began to close. Cy nodded and was gone.

Other than the sound of Nugget panting, the room was quiet as Vince propped up a couple pillows and started to get comfortable on the bed. Nugget continued to stare at Vince while he got situated and finally gave in.

"Come on, girl." Vince patted a spot next to him on the bed. That was the cue she'd been waiting for, and she leapt across the gap between the two beds. Finding a spot next to Vince, she rested her head on his leg. He scratched her behind the ears, and it was a welcome distraction for a while. He could feel his eyes growing heavy and he let himself slide down from his half-seated position until he was almost lying down. He tried to stay awake until Mary came out of the bathroom, but it was no use. The day's rigorous activities caught up with him and he drifted off to sleep.

At first, Vince thought he was dreaming, but the unmistakable sound of Mary's troubled voice and her hand on his arm brought him back to his senses.

"Vince. Vince, you've got to get up," Mary pleaded.

"What is it?" Vince squinted as his eyes struggled to focus on Mary's face in the darkness of the room. He could hear her quickened breathing and knew something was wrong.

"They're back," she answered.

Find out about Bruno Miller's next book by signing up for his newsletter:
http://brunomillerauthor.com/sign-up/

No spam, no junk, just news (sales, freebies, and releases). Scouts honor.

Enjoy the book?
Help the series grow by telling a friend about it
and taking the time to leave a review.

About the Author

BRUNO MILLER is the author of the Dark Road series. He's a military vet who likes to spend his downtime hanging out with his wife and kids, or getting in some range time. He believes in being prepared for any situation.

http://brunomillerauthor.com/

https://www.facebook.com/BrunoMillerAuthor/